CUT AND BRANDED

Dodge City—the end of the trail for the huge cattle herds being driven North and for many a cowpoke who tried to argue with a bullet. Stock detective Sam Benbow figured it was the logical last stop for 3,000 longhorns missing from the TRS ranch. He had a hunch who had rustled the herd and changed their brands. Now, he had just twelve hours to prove it before the train arrived, and the stolen steers shipped out as beefsteaks on the Kansas Pacific run.

But something else was rotten in Dodge. One by one the tribeless squaws camped on the city's riverbank were being sadistically murdered. As Benbow's memories turned to the past and an Araphoe maiden he once loved, a dangerous look came into his eye. To settle an old score he had to catch a killer, hang him high, shoot him down . . . or die himself in Dodge City.

Jack Curtis was born at Lincoln Center, Kansas. At an early age he came to live in Fresno, California. He served in the U.S. Navy during the Second World War, with duty in the Pacific theater. He began writing short stories after the war for the magazine market. Sam Peckinpah, later a film director, had also come from Fresno, and he enlisted Curtis in writing teleplays and story adaptations for *Dick Powell's Zane Grey Theater*. Sometimes Curtis shared credit for these teleplays with Peckinpah; sometimes he did not. Other work in the television industry followed with Curtis writing episodes for *The Rifleman, Have Gun, Will Travel,* Sam Peckinpah's *The Westerner, Rawhide, The Outlaws, Wagon Train, The Big Valley, The Virginian* and *Gunsmoke*. Curtis also contributed teleplays to non-Western series like *Dr. Kildare, Ben Casey* and *Four Star Theater*. He lives on a ranch in Big Sur, California, with his wife, LaVon. In recent years Jack Curtis published numerous books of poetry, wrote *Christmas in Calico* (1996) that was made into a television movie, and numerous Western novels, including *Pepper Tree Rider* (1994) and *No Mercy* (1995). *Lie, Eliza, Lie* will be published in 2002.

CUT AND BRANDED

Jack Curtis

GUNSMOKE

This hardback edition 2002
by Chivers Press
by arrangement with
Golden West Literary Agency

ISBN 0 7540 8183 4

British Library Cataloguing in Publication Data available.

Printed and bound in Great Britain by
BOOKCRAFT, Midsomer Norton, Somerset

For Wayne Hyland
Sea Man

The truth of art keeps science from becoming inhuman, and the truth of science keeps art from becoming ridiculous.

The Notebooks of Raymond Chandler,
Ecco Press, N.Y.

1

THE COMMANDER LOOKED MORE LIKE HE BELONGED ON a bakery shelf than in the office of the South Texas Cattlemen's Association. Built like a sugar bun, his round face wore the aspect of a floured ball of rising dough with lemon snap ears, but after that you saw the little gray eyes that were more like bullets than raisins.

His nose, mashed flat as a corn fritter in some youthful escapade, was more ornamental than useful. His small, doughnut-shaped mouth had to puff his breath in and out, which was maybe the reason he never said much.

An ungenerous, brilliant, conniving, farsighted son of a sea biscuit, he spent his spare time translating Dante's *Inferno,* which was the only time he ever laughed.

If you asked him who was the uncle of the grand duke of Russia, or how many kangaroos there were in Australia, or how much would a four-year-old Texas steer bring in Chicago that day, he would tell you the answer instantly, but he wouldn't go on and on about it.

Once on a hot August day I saw the blue fouled anchor tattooed on his pallid left forearm, which might have been related to his flattened nose. For sure he'd put that fritter nose in plenty of places besides books.

Otherwise, he was famous throughout Texas as a man who drank tea instead of coffee, Spanish brandy instead of whiskey, and beer instead of water.

"Water has had fish in it," he once said when I was trying to coax Skofer onto the stuff, ruining my whole lecture on the merits of cool, clear water over tepid, cloudy forty-rod.

The commander's family was still back in New England running shoe factories, being Supreme Court justices, or some such, but he avoided most of them unless he needed some special information they could provide.

All in all, he made a pretty fair boss because he came to work every morning on time and knew the business better than anyone else. When he said, "Fix the problem," he figured you would go ahead and fix it without having to hire half a dozen assistants to talk it over with.

He had a rare soft spot for my partner, Skofer Haavik, although he seldom showed it. Maybe because Skofer had once been a professor of divinity at the University of Virginia and then lost his faith during the war, or maybe because he was crusty and frail but still had spunk enough to hoot and howl when he was on a hoolihan. Whatever it was, I generally caught the blame for Skofer's high jinks, and Skofe was excused.

Bland-faced, the commander looked up at me as I stood in front of his desk and asked innocently, "Have a nice trip out west?"

"I fixed it," I said, figuring he had his own devious ways of counting the casualties.

"Then you're ready to go to work," he said, nodding.

"It wasn't much of a vacation." I made my little protest as a matter of form.

"Now we've got a nearly impossible theft problem," he said, disregarding my note of discontent. "Take poor old Skofer along."

"Do I get to know what, where, when, and how?"

"It's a herd of about three thousand Mexican cattle branded T R S connected," he said, drawing the brand on the back of an envelope:

"Off the Terrazas Ranch?"

"They're long gone north," he said with a nod. "Four months ago old Don Antonio sent a crew to drive them up to Dodge City. That was the last he heard of them."

"His vaqueros steal 'em?"

"No. All his herders were found gunshot near the border."

"Wants the cows back?" I asked.

"No, just the money." The commander smiled like a bulldog eyeing a porterhouse steak, then looked down at his pink hands, which was the signal for me to get moving and fix the problem.

All I had to do was find the cows, then take 'em away from a gang of gunmen who'd killed a dozen Mexican cowboys to steal 'em in the first place.

As I started for the door he remembered a little something extra.

"Just a second, Sam," he muttered. "There's been some strange killings up Dodge way. Don't get mixed up in them."

"You mean the dead-man-every-mornin'-for-breakfast kind of killin'?"

"No, I hear it's different." He looked down at his hands again.

Outside I found Skofer trying to teach a gray-muzzled street mongrel how to chase his ratty tail.

"C'mon, puppy dog," he crooned to the old mutt, swishing the end of the tail under his nose. "Sic 'em!"

The dog cocked his head and stared at Skofer.

"Skofe, that's an old dog."

"And I guess now you're going to tell me I can't teach him a new trick?" Skofer glared at me.

"No, I'm just sayin' when you're done with your experiment we can go hunt down some cows a couple thousand miles up the trail. No hurry."

"I don't think I can go that far without a drink," Skofer croaked in a weak, poor-me tone of voice that he used often enough to be forgettable.

"I can." I patted him on his bony shoulder.

"Say, now, isn't that a saloon?" Skofer squinted his eyes and pointed at the open door of the Brindle Bull Saloon, where he spent most of his time and all of my money.

Shaking my head sorrowfully, I pushed him through the batwing shutters. A simple place designed for men coming in off the range, it was unadorned except for the big brindle longhorn's head hanging on the back wall, which had been shot at various times and was festooned with odd mementos of forgotten hurrahs. Leap Malone, the bardog, frowned on punchers shooting the bull's head, but sometimes a high-flying cowboy was faster on the draw than Leap was with his sawed-off two-bore.

It was too early for bronc peelers or buckaroos to be bellying up to the bar, but for a change there were half a dozen federal troops getting an early start.

"Them's Seventh Cav," Skofer murmured. "Custer's bunch." Once Skofer had turned in his faith and joined up with Jeb Stuart, he learned his military markings well enough.

Of course, I'd rode alongside of him and picked up a few pointers as the years crashed on by.

We sidled over to the end of the bar out of harm's way, and when Leap Malone came mopping his trail up the greasy hickory planks I ordered a beer, and Skofer asked for whiskey.

"What's the commander say?" Skofer asked as Leap poured his glass full.

"Dodge City," I said. "Check on a Mexican brand, the T R S connected."

"That's the pretty one"—he smiled, showing his worn-down teeth—"all curlicues like a rooster fixin' to crow."

The troopers at the other end of the bar hadn't quit from the night before, from the looks of their lolling heads, red-veined eyes, and grim, stubbled faces.

A big-bellied blond sergeant next to me poured his drink from a half-empty bottle. Satisfied that the clear whiskey was at the proper level, he lifted his glass and yelled, "Here's to the Seventh!"

"Here's to the Seventh," his troopers grumbled, like they'd done this before.

"What did we do at the Washita?" he yelled.

"We killed 'em all! Ma and pa, at the Wash-i-ta!" his men responded.

"Where was the Seventh?" The sergeant held to the drill.

"In front, in front!" the men repeated.

"What did we do at the Wash-i-ta!"

"We killed 'em all, ma and pa, at the Wash-i-ta!"

"You damned right!" The burly sergeant smacked the bar top with the flat of his hand and glared around like a range bull in a ring.

"The human mind works in strange ways," Skofer murmured, tasting his drink. "What they're doin' is tryin' to forget what they're remembering."

"At Washita?" I asked quietly.

"You say something?" the blond sergeant growled at me. "Speak up!"

I shook my head and shrugged my shoulders, ready to leave. The last thing I wanted was a quarrel with these men, who were trying to live down what they'd done to several hundred defenseless men, women, and children.

"These men are all heroes!" the sergeant growled at me.

"Sure, Sergeant." I nodded, touching Skofer's elbow to get him moving.

"Don't talk down to me, mister!" The sergeant by now had sprouted the idea that he had to show what a battler he was.

"Look, Sergeant, we don't want a ruckus. We're leavin'."

"You ain't leavin' till you have a drink with me." He eyed me hard, brought his bottle over, and splashed some of the clear into my beer glass.

"Have a man's drink!" He grinned, showing his yellow teeth.

"I tried that once, and it blew pink steam out of my ears," I said, trying to cool him down.

He didn't like the joke.

"Drink up, old-timer," he growled, trying to smile at the same time. "Here, have a cigar."

From under his tunic he pulled out a pale, almost transparent case, open at one end, where it was fringed with a ruff of dry, curly black hair. It was just big enough to hold two cigars.

"No," Skofe said to me. He knew a lot more about my past than the sergeant did.

"I don't smoke," I said.

"You know what this is?" He grinned at me, his little red eyes probing.

"I know."

"Want to sniff it?" he guffawed, waving it under my nose.

"I reckon not."

He turned halfway around and yelled at his troopers, "What did we do at Wash-i-ta?"

"We scalped the squaws at Wash-i-ta!" they chorused, grinning foolishly.

Turning back to me, he said, "This one I scalped low, jerked out, and stretched on my saddle horn."

"No," Skofer said again.

"Why don't you give it a decent burial?" I murmured.

"Burial, hell! You tryin' to be smart?"

"Like I said, we're leavin'." I moved to step around him.

"Slow down, old horse," he said, his red eyes glistening. "You ain't had that drink yet."

"I'm not goin' to either, Sergeant."

He brought his right fist around as slow as a swinging gate, and as I stepped inside it I happily hooked him in the belly with my left. In my younger days that hook would have sandwiched him out the door, but this time he only staggered backward, clutching at his paunch with his right hand, his little red eyes still watching me close.

"You rebel son of a bitch," he gritted, and his right hand traveled a couple of inches to draw his holstered forty-four.

He knew I wasn't set right, but I had to try.

As my right hand caught the walnut grips of my Colt, Skofer threw the bottle, making his shot miss my left ear by a screech owl's whisker.

My 180-grain lead ball smacked him at the point of his wishbone, and the force of its velocity slammed him backward.

The revolver fell from his hand, and his little red eyes bulged with terror as he sank to his knees.

Leap Malone brought up his two-barrel, keeping the stunned troopers peaceable while Skofer and I moved toward the side door.

The sergeant let out a long rattling belch and started coughing up his life, what little there ever was of it.

2

THE COLORS OF AUTUMN, EVEN ON THE GREAT PRAIRIE where trees are absent except in marking the presence of water, were diffused by smoky golden light that enriched the tawny brown of the grama, galleta, and mesquite grasses. The stream banks, with their wild plums, cottonwoods, blackjacks, and ash groves, decorated the coppery bosom of the empty land like lazy loops of golden chain, accented by bright vermilion beads of hackberries and chokecherries.

Other than the occasional dished-out and grassed-over buffalo wallows and the clumped gray bones of the buffalo themselves, nothing disturbed the calm, smoky golden land. The Indians were gone, the buffalo hunters were gone, and the land waited like it was holding its breath before accepting the biting plows that were already being forged in Pittsburgh, Des Moines, or Chicago.

"Take a good look, Sam," Skofer said mournfully. "We'll never see it so fine again."

"You sound like old man winter already," I said, pointing the steeldust around the outskirts of a prairie-dog town.

He quoted gloomily:

"Then in a wailful choir the small gnats mourn
Among the river sallows, borne aloft
Or sinking as the light wind lives or dies."

"Don't you know any more Susan Van Dusan verses?" I tried to tease him out of his melancholy.

"None of those bawdy songs for this day," he said heavily. "This is a profound moment in the history of American civilization. We must savor it like a fine wine that can never be reproduced again."

Before I could start grumbling the long moan of a steam whistle came down on the breeze.

"You know what that means?" I asked.

"The end of the world as we know it," Skofer said lugubriously.

"No, it means that Dodge City is just over the rise." I pointed off toward a line of golden-leaved cottonwoods. "Those trees mark the Arkansas River."

"I'm too decrepit to drown my sorrows," Skofer muttered sadly. "Father Time has me by the elbow and leadeth me hence."

"I'm goin' to kick your butt hence in a minute," I said. "I would right now except I'm in a hurry."

"I deserve it, Sam. I haven't been much help on this trip."

"I haven't needed any help, you old idjit! Now put on a smile and think about all those barrels of Tennessee whiskey waitin' over yonder."

"Do you suppose they'll have such a divine potion this far out in the big nowhere?" He brightened up a little.

"I don't know why not." I kneed the steeldust into a fast trot. Off to the west were dust clouds where herds of Texas cattle were being grazed, waiting to go to market.

I hoped the Terrazas herd was among them.

As we came closer to the new cattle town the ground showed heavy travel and overgrazing from trailherds that had been coming through all summer.

We climbed a long, low hill and pulled up when we reached the crest.

Near a bend in the river lay the brand-new town of Dodge City, Kansas, which, from our view, looked like a jumble of shacks on either side of a dusty trail. Closer to the river was the Kansas Pacific Railroad, with a yellow frame building for a depot and a maze of plank and post cattle pens designed to funnel thousands of Texas cows into cattle cars ready to highball them to Chicago. Near the depot was a water tank on a tower for the steam engines, then the land curved down toward the river bottom, where it probably flooded in the spring.

On the outskirts of town were scattered hovels made of canvas and sod thrown together by newcomers to protect their goods and make a little shelter.

"Reckon there'll be any of the Seventh Cavalry hanging around?" Skofer asked.

"Possible. Fort Hays is just on west a ways."

"Supposin' they happen to recognize us?"

"The commander should have taken care of the legalities of that shooting. What are you worryin' about?" I asked.

"It don't hurt to worry a little once in a while," Skofer said heavily. "A stitch in time keeps the devil occupied."

"Skofe, this is a simple job," I said, exasperated with his pessimism. "We're goin' in and do it, then we'll decide whether to go on to California or go back to Austin."

I kneed the steeldust on down the broad trail that forded the low-running river, and as we splashed across I saw off to my left past the cattle pens a short street that seemed to be mainly saloons, gambling dens, and whorehouses, all hastily built and disguised with paint or remnants of bright cloth as elegant architecture. Further down, among the trees next to the river, was a garbage dump where the dregs of humanity huddled without any shelter at all. A few lumps of ragged derelicts lay in the shade, bottles clutched in their hands. Most of them were Indians.

"Skofer, you don't mend your ways," I said, "Johnny Barleycorn's goin' to put you right there."

"These folks have lost the fight," Skofer bristled, "but I have just begun."

The trail turned and went by the cattle pens nearly full of longhorns being moved through different gates and chutes toward the line of yellow cars on the siding.

Passing through the new Nauchtown, we crossed over the railroad tracks into the respectable side of Dodge, a city of no more than five hundred residents and maybe a thousand transient bug-eyed and spooked cowboys who'd become as wild as the longhorns they'd been driving for the past three or four months.

The first building on the right was made of burned brick, and a sign over the door said Gunther Shreich, M.D. Next to it was a gun- and locksmith named Elias Carter, then a couple of lawyers and a butcher shop called Spuds.

The other false-fronted buildings were mainly built of milled lumber hauled in by the railroad. The hitch rails next to the boardwalk were crowded with cow ponies, while newcomers rode down the street at a studdy trot, not sure if this was a safe place or not, ready to cut and run if they saw a decent woman or a trolley car, of which there were hardly any at that time.

Loaded freight drays moved away from the depot while empty ones took their places, and the clumping of star boot heels on the boardwalk sounded like an army going over a bridge. So far not a shot had been fired, although it was my inner feeling that the whole damn carnival was ready to blow its top.

Off down the side street I saw a shingled steeple, which meant that the forces of evil were at least being monitored by a Holy Joe.

Between saloons were a variety of stores selling harnesses, ladies' millinery, and general merchandise.

Down in the middle of all this busyness was the Drover's Inn, a boxy two-story building with a veranda on the front side.

We found space for the horses at the hitch rail and went inside.

"It's a good thing you came in early," the clerk said. "We're generally full by noon."

He was a thin young man with patches of red on his cheeks and a small waxed mustache. He looked consumptive to me, but that wasn't so strange. There was a lot of it going around, decimating the whites about as bad as the Indians.

We changed into our spare clothes after a hot bath in the copper tubs, and by then Skofer had gotten over his dark mood of the morning and was ready to take a switch to the bear.

I wouldn't let him loose, though, until we'd put the horses in the livery stable and seen they were fed. Then we went into Delmonico's Restaurant and had a dinner of liver and onions.

"You ready now?" I asked Skofer, feeling like I'd rather take a long nap than go to work.

"They say work will make you free," Skofe said drowsily.

"Who said that?"

"Schopenhauer or Münchhausen. Some Fritz meddler."

Two troopers came in the front door wearing blue tunics with yellow tape running down the sides of their pants.

"Yellow legs," I said, and I took a quick look to see if I knew their faces from Austin. I didn't recognize them.

One was short and slim, but he strutted like he was bigger'n pint-sized, and he wore an egret feather in his pinned-up hat brim.

The other was an average junior officer, too young to have fought in the war. I noticed that the banty rooster wore his yellow hair almost to his shoulders, and that he looked sharply around the room before sitting down.

"He's a ringer for Custer," Skofer murmured.

"But he's not George Armstrong," I said quietly.

"You know the general?" Skofer asked.

"No, but I saw him at Appomattox courthouse a few years ago. They made him a special place next to Grant because he was so good at burning down farmhouses."

"It's over," Skofer said softly. "Maybe we better start thinking about today."

I paid the bill, and we crossed behind the yellow legs and went out onto the boardwalk crowded with punchers who were anxious to go crazy or who had already gone crazy. Wasn't much difference.

I found the jail and the marshal's office across the street and down a block. Built of quarried limestone, it was a long, narrow building one story high.

The floor, made of flat slabs of limestone, already showed a trail from the front door to the desk at the back of the room. I figured the door by the desk would open on a couple of iron-barred cells.

Sitting behind the desk was a tall hump-shouldered man with a thick white mustache that looked like ragged Irish lace on the bottom side.

"Marshal?" I asked, looking into his cloudy gray eyes.

"Deputy," he said. "Deputy Fred Keogh. You want Marshal Earp, he's out of town."

"I'm interested in lookin' over the cattle outside of town," I said. "I was wondering if you happen to know their brands."

"We don't keep track of the brands goin' through the pens." Fred Keogh shook his head. "I've heard there's three, four herds on the holdin' grounds out west, but that's about it."

"This one would be from south of the border, and it's a brand that looks somethin' like this—"

I drew the brand with my finger in the dust on the desk:

"That's a new one for me."

From behind the door came a high, wailing voice, too rusty to be sweet-sounding and too high-pitched for comfort. The voice rose and fell in a strange rhythm, and it ran a shiver up my backbone.

I looked at Skofe, and he looked at the old deputy. "You got a dying Indian locked up back there?"

"The jury is still out." Fred Keogh nodded. "They'll probably hang him before sunset."

"Sounds like he already knows the jury's verdict," I said.

"The son of a bitch has been a pain in the butt ever since he drifted into town," Keogh said.

"You goin' to hang him for that?" I asked.

"I would, because I'm the one that's got to handle him whenever he breaks a window or steals a bottle, but I doubt if the rest would go that far."

"What'd he do?" Skofer put in.

"Been killin' those bums over by the river for quite a while. Folks got tired of hearin' about it. If it was me, I'd hang the whole bunch and get rid of the problem."

I remembered what the Commander had said: "There's been some strange killings . . . don't get mixed up in them."

"I guess we'll be runnin' along," I said before Skofer asked any more questions.

"What's your interest in that herd?" Keogh asked firmly before I could get Skofer turned around.

"We're just tryin' to see the right cows belong to the right brand," I said.

"Harmless enough." Keogh let his eyes go sleepy again.

"That's us," Skofer cackled. "We're more peaceable than old maids skinnin' skunks."

The wailing commenced again, and I said, "I guess we'll just leave you to your listenin' post, Mr. Keogh. Thank you kindly."

Outside, the whoops and hollers of cowboys bent

on being demented sounded better than the keening Indian, because it was more my kind of music.

Dodging staggering cowboys and an occasional begging Indian outcast, we walked down the boardwalk to a big frame building with a fancy false front that announced itself in big red letters as the New Elephant Saloon.

Inside, the sawdust on the floor was no fresher than most such places, and the layout was the same, with the bar running across the back and round tables and oak chairs filling up the front part. A few sporters sat closest to the door, but it was early in the day, and they hadn't reached their peak of enthusiasm yet. Their faces sagged in the daylight like watery mashed potatoes. Even their feathers looked poorly.

I let Skofer lead the way through the tangle of cowboys coming and going, because he's an expert at barroom scouting.

The bartender was another stamped-out copy with his waxed mustache curled up and pink garters holding up his shirt-sleeves. The apron he had tucked around his ample midriff had seen better days as a flour sack.

I ordered a beer, and Skofer quickly said, "Give me the best whiskey in the house."

The rubicund bartender drew my beer, then reached a bottle of clear off the back bar, the same as everyone else was drinking, and poured the squat glass full without spilling a drop.

Skofer looked at the clear glass carefully and shook his head sadly.

"You'd think if mankind could invent a steam engine, it could figure how to haul whiskey from Tennessee."

"You'd think if mankind could invent whiskey, it could invent a cure for it, too," I said.

"Who the hell wants a cure?" Skofer demanded, downing the drink and shuddering like a wet dog.

"Them people that see snakes and such usually want a cure of some kind."

"That's because they don't know the meaning of moderation," Skofer said, shoving the empty glass forward and rapping on the bar with a silver dime.

"It's some early for you to fire up the boiler," I said mildly, knowing it was useless to say anything at all.

The truth of it was that Skofer was about the same kind of a drunk as most down-and-out derelicts were. He was just lucky that his friends took care of him. He couldn't change. I'd seen him try and fail enough times to understand there was a thirst in him that he had no name for. If he couldn't figure out what it was, he couldn't hardly beat it.

Far as I was concerned, sticking through four years of the bloodiest warfare ever in America gave him a free pass to do any damned thing he wanted to, short of murder.

On down the bar I recognized Joe McCoy, the cattle broker I'd known in Abilene. He was talking to a rounded-out, elegantly dressed big man who wore a full, glossy black beard as if to compensate for the hairless skull that gleamed and showed the bone fissures underneath.

On down the bar stood the young banty rooster cavalryman talking to a big slope-shouldered man in greasy buckskins.

"Is that General Custer?" I asked the bartender quietly.

"His brother, Tom," the bartender said under his breath without moving his lips.

"That's what fooled me," I nodded.

"That's old Liver Eater Maric with him," the bartender added in the same nonexistent voice.

I put a cartwheel on the bar and asked, "Anybody else famous I ought to know?"

"The man with McCoy calls himself Baron Alexis Nabokov. That's free." The bartender smiled.

"Is he really a baron?" I asked, puzzled more than awed.

"I hear he's some kind of Russian nobleman's woods colt that was sent over here for family pride."

I knew nothing about Baron Nabokov, but Liver Eater Maric had made himself famous years ago when he and some trappers met a band of marauding Crow Indians. Maric's entire family had been clubbed to death by some other Indians about a year before, and the story went that he was still so crazy, he caught a wounded Crow brave and, in front of friends and enemies, sliced him open and ate his liver raw as the worst possible revenge a man could do to an Indian. Whether he ate any more livers after that I never heard, but one was enough to give him the sobriquet of Liver Eater Maric forever more.

Of course, with Tom Custer he was in good company, because there was no secret about the Custers' intentions toward redskins.

I recognized John Slaughter and Print Olive, both Texas cattlemen, and then I saw Wagon Tongue Nellie, one of Skofer's old flames, sit down with the sporters.

"Your luck has changed and your day has come," I said to Skofer, who was eyeing another full glass on the bar like it was about to bite him unless he grabbed a choke hold on it first.

He followed my eyes and shook his head. "That's the one that borrowed my life's savings," he grumbled.

"My savings," I corrected him. "You took my money and gave it to her, remember?"

"She promised to triple it in a week," he said, nodding.

"I remember. She was goin' to buy leftover Union uniforms cheap in the north and sell them high in Texas."

"Well, everybody needs clothes," Skofer grumbled.

"Some Texans still remember the blue." I shook my head. "I'm surprised you didn't get us lynched."

At a large table near the door, a group of serious-minded citizens dressed like merchants finished off the second of two bottles on the table, and the man with the roundest jowls stood up and rapped the table with the empty bottle until the crowd quieted down.

"That's Kennefik the banker," the barman murmured quietly.

"Gentlemen of Dodge City, the pride of the prairie and the safest place in all America, we have arrived at a verdict."

His eyes, slick as wet soap, traveled over the crowd, and he smiled like he was doing everybody a favor.

"We have found Chief Strike Axe guilty of all the killings down at the river camp, and the sentence is that he be hanged by the neck until dead."

"That'll teach the son of a bitch a lesson he won't forget!" a wobbly cowboy sang out.

"Up-and-comin' little town," I said to Skofer. "You want to watch?"

"Not me." Skofer shook his head. "Me 'n' old Wagon Tongue have got some business to catch up on."

"I hope you don't catch what I think you're goin' to catch," I said, drifting along after the crowd.

By the time the jury reached the jail, half the town was in the audience. It was all so cut and dried, most of the excitement was hushed down, and some of the wiser ones remembered they had better things to do, like mending boots or currying the family horse.

Deputy Keogh offered no argument, and the townsmen emerged from the jail with a short, fat

Indian, maybe a Comanche or Kaw, dressed in ragged discards. His long hair was matted with sandburs, and he hadn't washed recently. His eyes were too close together and slightly crossed. From the foolish smile on his face, I thought he might be a little short of furniture in the upstairs parlor, or else Fred Keogh had slipped him a farewell bottle.

As Keogh stepped clear of the group the burly town butcher—who must have been Spud himself, from the looks of his bloody apron—and another jasper in regular trail-riding clothes grabbed Strike Axe by the arms and started him down the street.

"Whereaway?" someone yelled.

"How about the water tower?"

Keogh came alongside and said, "Like the show?"

"The clowns are pretty good," I said with a nod. "Who's that eager one on the chief's left arm?"

"Rafe Egan. Trail driver. Used to make a living in Texas collecting bounty on Indian scalps until they caught him including Mexican hair."

A couple others in the crowd who seemed out of place puzzled me.

"That one in the old army uniform?"

"Ex–Major Fred Hawes. His troops were whipped by a war party of Cheyennes, and the brass cashiered him for it."

"The other one with the sombrero and long hair?"

"Moon Gould," Keogh murmured. "He was scout for the major. I heard he ran when he saw the war party instead of reporting back."

"Looks like old Strike Axe has plenty of friends willing to adjust his necktie."

"More than enough, even though everybody knows he could never have done what the killer did," Keogh said agreeably.

Near the railroad tracks Moon Gould, with a coil of hemp slung over his shoulder, climbed up the trusswork that supported the water tank.

Passing the rope over a timber that extended out from the tower, Gould stared down at the crowd for a second, his gaunt face looking like a skull with a candle burning behind each eye; then he dropped back down to the ground. He expertly made a hangman's knot as the butcher rolled up a high-wheeled baggage cart. With the butcher helping, Gould hoisted Strike Axe up on the splintered planks and slipped the noose over his head.

Strike Axe smiled like a trained bear that's learned if you smile long enough, maybe someone will give you something.

"Swing, you goddamned ripping bastard!" someone yelled.

From out of the crowd a small, wiry townman dressed in a black suit stepped forward, raised his right hand in protest, and cried out in a Germanic accent, "Don't do this barbaric thing!"

"He's been judged guilty, Doc!" the jowly Kennefik responded.

"There is no guilt anymore," the doctor came back strongly.

"Who's the voice from the cellar?" I asked Keogh.

"Doc Schreich. He's been around awhile." Keogh smiled.

"What the hell are you waitin' for?" the major yelled, and immediately Egan, Gould, and the butcher leaned against the cart and sent it rolling out from underneath Strike Axe.

Mercifully for the audience, the rope broke his larynx first. I didn't stay to watch him kick.

— 3 —

SKOFER'S SNORE STARTED AS A GENTLE RATTLE AS IF from some small sidewinder tuning up in dry leaves, then grew in volume like a freight train gathering speed to make it up over the next hill. Once on the crest it sounded like a thirsty spaniel slopping up water from a bowl, then changed into a descending clucking sound in the manner of a hen with chicks. At the end of the inhalation he paused, changed pipes, and commenced a withdrawing sibilance forming a melody akin to "Flow Gently Sweet Afton," ultimately ending in a piping arpeggio suitable for piccolo.

His open mouth showed his worn-down teeth, and his face was the gray-greenish color of swamp mud.

He'd managed to get one boot off before tumbling onto the cot sometime in the night.

Streaks of red lip rouge across the front of his shirt indicated that Wagon Tongue Nellie had marked the bill Paid in Full.

On the way over to Delmonico's for breakfast I heard the clatter of a switch engine over by the cattle pens and the bawling of cattle being driven where they didn't want to go.

An occasional whipped cowboy slumped in a doorway, sleeping off the poison he'd taken as ambrosia the night before. Stray dogs prowled the boardwalk and rolled in the piles of wet horse manure on Main Street.

Delmonico's was quiet. A few early-rising cattlemen and a storekeeper were having their morning coffee at the counter, and I sat on a stool next to a railroader wearing striped overalls and a striped cap with a bill.

We exchanged good mornings, and after I'd ordered breakfast he asked, "What was all that ruckus down by the water tank yesterday?"

"They hung an Indian," I said, wishing I'd been lucky and picked another seat.

"What'd he do?" the railroader asked eagerly.

"Nobody seems to be sure."

The storekeeper on the other side of the railroader pointed his sharp nose into the conversation and said, "He killed a bunch of squaws down at the river camp."

"Anybody see him do it?" the railroader asked.

"He was the only one down there with a knife,"

the storekeeper said. "And he did it the hard way, too."

"How's that?" The railroader licked his lips.

The storekeeper looked around the room, bent his head in close, and whispered, "He cut out their organs. He'd cut a T in the belly and jerk 'em out."

"Holy cow!" The railroader whistled. "Wait'll I tell that in Chicago!"

I looked at my slab of ham and two-eyed eggs and told myself I must clean my plate or I would get no pie.

"Been goin' on for some time?" I asked.

"Six months or so." The storekeeper nodded wisely. "He'd eviscerate one a month, on average."

"Was any of 'em . . . molested?" the railroader whispered.

"Them ugly old greasy squaws? Not likely!" The storekeeper grinned.

"How many'd he get all told?"

"Seven at the last count. Nobody would have minded if he'd just thrown 'em in the river, but he always left a mess for somebody to clean up, and there's the damn buzzards down there, too. That's what got him hung," the storekeeper said righteously.

"Just seven . . ." The railroader frowned like he'd hoped for a bigger number to make the story better in Chicago.

I decided I could skip the pie.

"Hey, you didn't eat your breakfast," the railroader protested when I stood up to pay my bill.

"I'm tryin' to lose weight," I said, and I went on outside into the clean morning.

Not a bad idea, I thought. Quit eating breakfast, lose ten pounds, get your belt buckle up where it used to be. You'd look less like a horsehair-stuffed mattress, and all the girls would look at you sideways and put the wiggle in the jiggle.

Nothing like clean, wholesome thoughts to cheer a man up, I decided, walking toward the railroad yard, imagining pretty, pert little behinds wiggling at slim Sam.

Draymen with their heavy wagons were arriving at the freight dock and loading up with lumber and kegs of nails, horseshoes, whiskey, cast-iron stoves, and boxed goods. An Indian squaw with matted long black hair, wearing a cast-off cotton blanket tied around her fat belly with a length of twine, staggered out of the shadows and, looking at the ground, held out her hand and mumbled, "Money? Money?"

"Why aren't you on the reservation?" I asked.

"No like," she mumbled. "Money? Like money."

"Better you go back to your own people."

"No people. You want fuckee? Two bits."

I gave her the quarter and watched her stumble away on her own pitiful path.

Climbing up the heavy timbers that railed the cattle pen, I gazed over a sea of tossing horns and hides of many colors dappling the shifting surface. The bawling drowned out the noise of the switch engine moving loaded cars to the train they were making up.

The brands I saw were Circle Ms, Crow Tracks,

and Wine Cups, which I recognized from neighboring ranches outside of San Angelo. They must have put their cows together for the drive north because all of them were road-branded with a long Lazy X.

All fair and legal. In four days they'd be beefsteaks.

I climbed back down to hard ground and walked over to the shipping office, where the tally books were kept. A yellow-painted board-and-batten building with a front porch, it looked like it had become a customary place for cattlemen to meet and discuss business, sharing information about the trail, the trend of prices, the condition of cattle, their diseases, parasites, and problems.

Several oak railroad chairs were set back against the wall, and some old Chicago newspapers lay on a rickety table. I noticed they were all turned to the Chicago Board of Trade page, where the latest commodity prices were printed. Scattered around the chairs were curly white pine shavings that some earnest whittlers had produced as they sat around and talked cows.

From the porch's elevation a man had a good view of the pens and the cattle, and I supposed there would be a barefoot boy handy to run and fetch for the tough old ranchers.

I took a newspaper and settled back in the nearest chair.

Yearlings brought ten dollars and feeder steers twenty-five to thirty dollars a head. That was down a bit from the year before but still plenty high to make rich men out of war-poor, raggedy-ass Texans.

Three thousand stolen Terrazas cattle would bring at least $75,000, which was not exactly goober peas.

The office door swung open, and Joe McCoy, the broker who'd built Abilene and was now moving his operation to Dodge, came out with the big bearded bear of a man called Baron Nabokov.

Being acquainted with McCoy from two years before, I stood up to shake hands. He was a slim, bony gent with a face that reminded me of pictures of the devil with his sharp nose and high cheekbones. But there was little or no deviltry in McCoy; he was always the serious businessman trying to make his imagination pay off.

"How are you, Benbow?" he asked. "Still working as a brand inspector?"

Something tickled the back of my neck, and I lied. "No, I quit. Now I'm lookin' around for where the money is."

"I told you to do that last time we talked." McCoy smiled by pressing his lips together tightly. "Let me introduce you to Baron Alexis Nabokov."

I turned to shake hands with the barrel-chested, bearded man and looked into his dark brown eyes. All I saw were ice caves.

"The Baron is going to start a beef packing operation here in Dodge. Maybe you and he can do some business."

"Pleased," the baron said, meeting my grip but adding nothing extra.

"You mean move the butchering and packing out here to the beef?"

"It would be a new and efficient way of doing it," the baron said with a strong guttural accent.

"Takes a lot of capital, I reckon," I said. "You'd need plenty of ice and special railroad cars."

"You're right," the Baron said. "We are forming a company now in order to raise that capital."

"Might be a place for me in that kind of operation," I said. "One thing I know is cows."

"You ought to hire him on as general manager right now, Baron," McCoy said seriously. "Benbow won't let you down."

I felt sorry I'd lied to him.

"We can't hire anyone just yet." The baron smiled, his big, square face open as a punkin pie. "Not until we have you included in the company as executive vice president."

"No, thank you, Baron. I don't have time for another job." McCoy pinched his lips together again in a smile.

"But there is no work to it. Only the title." The baron laughed. "Once the investors see your name on the executive board, they will all rush forward to join us."

"I couldn't do that until I've read all the documents." McCoy shook his head. "That might take me a month. Better make Benbow your executive vice president. He'll serve the company well."

"But I'm afraid not many people know Mr. Benbow's name," the baron said. "Isn't it enough that I put up my whole herd as good-faith collateral?"

"It's a generous offer, Baron." McCoy nodded and went on down the steps. "We'll talk about it later if I can get free."

"Fine. There is no hurry," the baron said, following along. "My cattle are only getting fatter every day I wait."

They said their courtesy good-byes and left me with a week-old newspaper.

I wondered about putting a packing plant out this far west. Maybe it'd work, maybe not. It depended, like most businesses, on how good the management was once it was started. From what the baron said, it looked like it'd take at least a million dollars to build a first-class plant. Of course, anything could go wrong, like a money panic in the east, a new railroad running down into the middle of Texas, a tick fever or cholera scare, the northern ranges beating out the tough longhorns with meatier shorthorn cattle—lots of things could go wrong with the business, and that's probably why Joe McCoy was reluctant to join in.

The baron was perfectly correct when he'd said the investors would back McCoy because he was known to be hardworking, inventive, and honest. He was a proven money maker, and I'd never heard an unkind word said about him.

I went into the office and asked the young clerk for a list of brands that were waiting out on the prairie to be sold and shipped.

"We never know for sure what all is out there," the young clerk replied, trying not to be officious. "They're still coming up from the south, so we don't have a complete record."

He showed me a sort of ongoing log of herds whose owners had come in and talked about selling, but there was little to go on except the brands, ear crops, and owners.

John Slaughter had a herd of Double-Mill Irons with a left ear over hack.

Print Olive had a Bar O with a right ear steeple-fork.

Baron Alexis Nabokov's herd was branded a Frying Pan with a grub right ear. Nelson Story's herd was branded NS with a left split ear. S.F. Coffey's herd was branded Rocking Chair with a steeple fork left ear.

Each herd would move according to its selling arrangements with McCoy or other commission men, and the long line of Texas longhorns would keep on coming to fill the constantly moving cattle cars.

Nothing on that list suggested the intricate Moorish-style Terrazas brand or its right ear underslope.

I thanked the clerk, moseyed on outside, and on a hunch went over to the telegraph office, where a lanky jasper with fine tan hair clamped under a green eyeshade sat at his key.

"Something?" he asked.

I wrote a message on a form, addressed it to C. L. Frazier, Austin, Texas, and handed it over.

"KEEP BARON ALEXIS NABOKOV IN MIND FOR GRAND PRIZE," he read out loud, and added, "You on the Committee for Social Betterment?"

"Chairman," I said.

He gave me a look sour as a bucket of last week's camel pee and muttered, "Cost you a dollar."

After I paid him I walked back past the cattle pens toward the river.

The code was simple enough to start the commander pulling in information about the baron from all over.

Along the way broken bottles—brown, green, blue, and clear—lay scattered like a carpet of jewels in the sunlight. The town's garbage went to feed the pigs and chickens in people's backyards.

Closer to the river amongst a grove of old cottonwoods the lumpy pariah Indians camped out. Half dressed in dirty rags, they huddled in the shade.

Their eyes, stupefied by rotgut, were almost opaque, their hair lousy and filthy, their faces battered, sometimes with unattended open cuts swarming with flies.

As I paused before each one of the women I heard the same whining litany, "Money . . . money . . . fuckee . . . two bits . . ."

The men kept it simple: "Money . . . money . . ."

One of them, a gaunt starvation case with one eye, said, "Me chief . . . money . . . money . . ." and offered me his nearly empty pint bottle. It smelled like a rat had drowned in the barrel. I passed the bottle back to him and went on to the next lump of mud in rags.

She looked up at me with her glazed dark brown eyes and said, "Money . . . money . . . fuckee two bits . . ."

"Why are you here?" I asked. "Why aren't you with your people?"

"No people. No buffalo. No eat. No place."

"The government agency?" I persisted, thinking I'd known a lady that looked something like this one when I was a roving kid in Colorado early on.

"Him steal all. No give eat. All die."

"Are you an Arapahoe?"

"I am Arapahoe," she said, a touch of pride left in her voice.

She looked more like the grandmother of a girl called Spring, the girl I'd married a thousand years ago before the war, when I was a young bronco looking for adventure.

"Is your name Spring?"

"No . . ." She hesitated, bothered by some recollection of the name, and looked away.

"Spring?" I asked gently.

"My name Satin Dancer," the lumpy-faced woman said. "Money . . . money . . . fuckee two bits . . ."

"Do you know the Valley of Many Mink?" I tried again.

She closed her eyes and rocked back and forth on her big butt. "Heap fuckee two bits . . ." she chanted.

I wanted to ask her if she knew anything about the killings, but she pulled a small bottle of tobacco-colored alcohol from between her legs and, with both shaking hands on the bottle, took a drink.

Putting the bottle back under her skirt, she smiled and showed the gaps in her teeth. "Good! Heap good!"

She wasn't Spring, even though her eyes were similar. Maybe lots of squaws had those same wide brown eyes with the slight tilt upward above the cheekbone.

The next woman didn't have eyes like that. Her eyes were scummed over from some terrible disease, and I tried to walk on by, but she heard me and held out her twisted hand. "Money . . . money . . ."

I put a quarter in the hand, and right away the one-eyed chief crawled over to rob her. I pushed him down flat and said, "No!"

"She dead," he said, frowning at me like I was stupid.

"You're all dead," I said, trying to think of some way I could give them back their lives.

On Main Street, still wondering if the woman called Satin Dancer was a relative of Spring or not, I saw the resplendent Tom Custer—egret feather, shining saber, and gold braid frogs on his blue cloak—strutting up the street, showing the lower peasants what a fine peacock he was.

He did pretty well at it. People got out of his way. Women clutched at their bodices, ready to swoon. Youngsters watched him with wide-eyed admiration.

I thought he looked silly, but then maybe deep down I wished I had all that ferocious dash and style.

His gauntlets were made of fringed doeskin, and his left hand rested on the brass saber guard while he seemed to be scanning the horizon for hostiles.

He was so busy looking over the heads of the foot traffic that he missed the Indian woman in the doorway of the saddle shop. She waited until he was almost past, then stepped forward and put both her hands on his right arm.

"Tomm-ee!" she called out. "Money . . . money . . ."

He glared at her and tried to shake loose, but she hung on.

"Tomm-ee . . . money . . ." she cried out again. Though slender, she wasn't quite as used up as the other begging squaws.

"Let go!" he commanded, trying to shake her off.

"Tomm-ee, you no remember?" She tried a coy smile and a soulful eye on him, which only made him madder.

Red-faced and with bulging eyes, he hit her in the face with a fair left hook strong enough to stun her.

"No remember fuckee, Tomm-ee?" she cried out, letting loose her grip on his arm. She smiled and pulled her blanket aside, cupped her flabby breast in her hand, and pointed the dark nipple at him. "Suckee more?"

People stopped to watch, curious as to what would happen next. In true Custer style, he didn't wait to think it over.

With his right fist he hit her three more times in the face, so fast the moves were a single blur.

She slumped slowly, but he wasn't finished. He hit her with the left hook again and then dropped an overhand right on her forehead.

As she crumpled on the boardwalk he brought his booted right leg back to kick her in the belly.

What's a man to do? Me, or any man who has to

live with himself and is faced with intimidation by a man in uniform? "A man's a man for a' that," Bobby Burns said, and I reckon that says it.

With all that settled in my mind a long time ago, I lost no time in getting my own right hand across. It landed high on Custer's neck because I was off balance and only wanted to get him away from the sobbing woman.

He wasn't hurt, and he could have cooled off and let bygones be bygones, but pride was playing its old tricks on him, and he couldn't bear to see himself as a mortal human being with maybe less brains than most.

He stepped back and squared away at me. I expected a rush, but I was still hoping he'd think some and avoid it.

Hell, it was common knowledge that he and his brother, George Armstrong, and the other senior officers of the Seventh took their pick of the prettiest Indian girls after every battle and installed them in their tents until they were tired of them.

Deep down, folks didn't much like the idea, but after all, the Custer boys deserved the best, didn't they? And anyway, the girls were lucky to still be alive.

From this I reckoned that somewhere in Tom Custer's makeup would be a little practical horse sense, but instead of backing up or making a rush he drew his pearl-handled Colt forty-four and pointed it right at my big nose.

"Who the hell are you?" he demanded, "and what gives you the right to intervene in my affairs?"

This is exactly the way he talked. You might as well say he was a fool carrying a gun.

"Get movin'," I said.

"By God, I will teach you to mind your own business!"

His knuckle whitened on the trigger while I decided my only chance was to dive off to my left into the crowd of petrified onlookers.

I wouldn't have made it, but I was going to try, when the squaw lurched upward against his left side.

The trigger pulled, but the shot went by my ear.

I hit him square on the nose with my right and grabbed the six-gun with my left, forcing his hand down so that he would shoot his own foot if he pulled that trigger again.

I hit him in the face again with a clubbing right that put a big blue blister under his left eye.

He struggled gamely, but I had the weight, and I wasn't nervous about using it so long as he still held on to the Colt.

"Give me that gun, you little pissant," I gritted out, trying to squeeze his gun hand into jelly.

"Like hell," he said tightly, then he smiled as he looked over my shoulder.

Even with your hat on, a gun barrel crowning your head can be an unpleasant surprise with aftershocks. It feels like your brain has been smashed into two parts, and both of them are slamming against the top of your skull. It makes you sick at the stomach, nearly blind, and flabby in the muscles. Two such licks are worse.

I counted three before I went down on my knees,

but I managed to partially block the third blow by putting my left wrist in the way.

"It's him!" someone yelled in my ear. "The one from Austin!"

I got a glimpse of big clenched fists coming out of army-blue sleeves, and then it got worse. There were two of them batting me back and forth like a rubber ball while the captain watched with a warm smile.

"Make it three ways, Corporal," I thought I heard someone say, then I saw the lashing right hand of Tom Custer coming at my head.

Round and round we go, as they say, and it was quite a ride.

I didn't know the corporal or the other one, I only knew Custer, and I made up my mind that the next time around I was going to catch the brass ring.

I let my hands down and slipped my head away from their blows to minimize their force. Then, coming into the dim view of my right eye, I saw the golden-haired lad, one of the heroes of the Washita, and I brought up my best uppercut to smash just under his pointed chin.

His head snapped back, and, reeling backward, he collapsed in the mounds of fresh horse manure.

I turned too late as one of the others hit me over the head again with his gun barrel. Fading away, I tried to break my fall with my arms, but as the darkness came down on me I never landed.

Someone was holding me up, and I heard a familiar voice grating, "Enough! Get out of my town, and don't come back!"

"He hit the captain!"

"I said git, and take little fancy-pants with you, too," Deputy Fred Keogh said harshly.

"Wait till the general hears about this!" the corporal replied sharply. "This man killed our sergeant down in Texas."

"I haven't seen a warrant."

"If he killed Sergeant McGuane, I promise you the Seventh will level this town and hang him!" Tom Custer sounded like a terrier barking at a cat up a tree.

"Captain, sir," the corporal interrupted, "it won't happen. We just came from Fort Hays to tell you the Seventh has been posted up to Wyoming Territory. The general's in a hurry."

"Goin' to try to break the Sioux?" Keogh asked.

"We'll exterminate them!" Custer chuckled.

"Be sure to catch 'em all in bed—especially the women and children," I murmured as the last little light in my head dimmed and my knees gave way.

4

I WOKE UP WITH THE SMELL OF IODINE, ETHER, CARBOLIC acid, vinegar, and coal-oil lamps in my nose and the steady crashing of boxcars being shunted through the echoing roundhouse of my brain. I stared at the white-painted ceiling and winced as iron banged against iron.

If I was an Indian, they'd call me Ironhead. I thought maybe a little humor might soothe the train wreck in my skull, but it only made it worse.

I promised it I would never smile again.

"Posted to Wyoming Territory," someone had said. Made sense. They'd sent the sergeant and his company down to Austin to buy remounts for the campaign against the Sioux. Now they were on their way to hell and gone and wouldn't be ragging me about the sergeant anymore. That made us almost even.

From the other side of the room I heard casual noises unrelated to freight trains. A scrape of a chair on the floor, throat clearing, yawning, glassware tinkling. Soft fingers touched my wrist and pressed down.

"How is he, Doc?"

I recognized one of Skofer's voices, the one he uses on hopeless cases.

"Pulse normal. No change, really," said the voice I remembered protesting the chief's hanging.

"I'm going down the street for a cup of coffee," Skofer said. "If he gets worse, let me know."

"It chust takes time, Mr. Haavik," the doctor said in his heavy Germanic accent. "If there's a blood clot, he may be paralyzed or expire. If there's only minor concussion, then he'll just have a massive headache."

"I hate to wish a headache on a friend," Skofer said, "but in this case I do."

"I suppose you believe in prayer?" the doctor asked neutrally.

"Not often. I saw too many bodies of boys stacked up in the mud at Shiloh," Skofer said. "You?"

"I'm a scientist, Mr. Haavik. Trained in Germany," the doctor murmured. "I have eliminated deities and superstition from my lexicon."

"I guess we've arrived at the same place, but we come by different roads to get there," Skofer said, and I heard the door open and close.

I tried the view of the ceiling again. It seemed to be

whiter. More light. Why? Sun coming up, maybe. Maybe moon. What was I supposed to be doing? Find Terrazas cows before they went to the packing house where cows walked in and came out meat.

The cattle cars were moving day and night, disappearing the cows. How long before the Terrazas bunch would go east? How much time did I have to find them?

I tried wiggling my toes, but without seeing them, I couldn't tell. They say a man with his arm cut off still feels it's there. Maybe I was paralyzed and didn't know it yet. That'd make me some salty, I thought, but just thinking hurt too much. I quit it and closed my eyes again.

"I saw your big toe move, Mr. Benbow. Was that intentional or reflexive?" the doc asked.

"Me," I whispered.

"Excellent."

I opened my eyes again and looked up at the wiry, rumpled doctor leaning over me. He was balding in the front, so his forehead looked like a massive, glistening dome full of knowledge. His overgrown eyebrows were black and twisted up at the ends like woolly horns. The bespectacled eyes were inquisitive, studying my face, probably observing color, breathing, skin dry or sweated, eyes dull or bright. His nose was long and made a sharp spine down the middle of his pouchy face. His Teutonic jaw was set solid, like he had no doubts at all about his medicine —or his life, for that matter.

"I was afraid the skull might have been fractured," he said quietly. "You took some severe blows."

"Where am I?" I asked. "What happened?"

"Excuse me. I'm Dr. Gunther Schreich. You're in my examination room. You were in an altercation yesterday afternoon und received a severe concussion. You are now on the road to recovery." A small smile touched his lips, as if he were pleased with his own succinct report.

"Thanks, Doc. What do I do now?" I asked, feeling weak, queasy, and miserable.

"Chust rest. A few more hours here und then you can go back to the hotel und lie down."

"There's things need doin'," I muttered.

"No, sir. I specify complete rest. If your blood pressure goes up, you may well suffer an aneurysm, und"—he snapped his fingers—"that would be that."

"We don't want that to be that." I tried and failed to make my fingers snap like his. "Do we?"

"I could give you some ethyl ether that'll put you to sleep," he said firmly, "but I dislike giving drugs in the case of cranial trauma."

"I'll be good," I said, lifting my right hand to calm his worries.

I'd been given opium in the war when I was shot, and I took a liking to it whether I was in pain or not. I'd rather snooze and dream pretty pictures than eat. Then I found how hard it was to quit.

I closed my eyes and took a deep breath. I didn't want to start again.

"You spoke up against that hangin' yesterday," I said.

"I wish I could have stopped it." Doc nodded. "It

was without logical foundation. He was obviously innocent."

"Made a convenient scapegoat for somebody," I murmured.

"True enough, but hanging Strike Axe solved no problem. I have no doubt that the killings will continue."

"Why?"

"Someone in the area is deranged. Someone seeking revenge subjectively. Someone who bears a grudge against all Indians."

"There's a lot of them."

"I would tend to agree," he said, "not that the killings themselves have significance."

"I suppose they're significant to the squaws."

"In the drugged state they're in, I doubt if even they care. I've read studies on aborigine mental capacity, and due to their heritage they are not much more intelligent than a jackrabbit."

"You talkin' about schoolin'?" I asked, trying to understand what he was saying.

"No, I'm speaking of the Indians' capacity for intellectual thought compared to whites'. Most scientists blame it on their ancestral environment. Q.E.D.: If I don't think, I am not." He chuckled like a chipmunk with hiccups.

"Still, they're human."

"We would have to define human first," he said. "What seems human to us might not to them, and vice versa."

We were bogged down in four-dollar words that

you could keep splitting into different meanings until everything turned gray.

"Don't misunderstand me," he added. "I wish them well, but they are a race doomed to extinction simply because the accident of ancestry makes them useless in the modern world."

"Whatever's right, Doc." I nodded, feeling confused and very tired.

"Rest," he said softly as I drifted off again.

Skofer's high-pitched squawk woke me later on in the morning. This time my headache had diminished to the more normal beating of a bass drum between my ears.

When I opened my eyes he was standing beside the doctor, trying to look worried but unable to keep the smile off his gnarly face.

"You don't travel like a colt no more, old-timer," he croaked.

I didn't need anybody to remind me.

"Doc says you can walk over to the hotel soon as your legs can carry you."

"You could stay here," Doc Schreich said apologetically, "but I'm running behind on my regular work."

I swung my legs over and got my feet on the floor. Skofer found my boots and pushed them on while I fought through a dizzy spell he didn't know anything about.

It didn't get any easier when I stood on my own, but after half a minute all the doors wavering around combined into one, and I headed that way.

"Much obliged, Doctor," I said.

We were almost to the front door of the hotel when Deputy Keogh came out and stopped to look me over.

"Close to ruint," he said, his old gray eyes keen, his spare shoulders still bowed over. He didn't look nearly as hard a man as he deep down was.

"I thank you for your help," I said. "I needed it bad just then."

"In my judgment," he said, "all them Custers is arrogant dog turds."

"They left?"

"Supposed to have gone north at daybreak."

"I remember some," I said.

"There's more if you're up to it," he drawled slowly, frowning like he wasn't sure if he was doing the right thing or not.

"Shoot."

"Was another squaw killed last night down at the river camp."

I thought it over and muttered, "That gives Strike Axe an alibi."

"A little late."

"Same knife work?"

"I can't figure the mind of a man who'd do that," he said with a nod. "Once they're dead, why cut out the lower belly?"

"Makes his mark, like it's a signature." I shrugged my shoulders. "It wasn't that woman that grabbed on to young Custer?"

"No, it was another one, went by the name of Satin Dancer."

"Goddammit," I said, and I chewed on my upper lip to keep quiet.

"Know her?" Keogh asked sharply.

"Some," I said, and I went on by him.

Skofer stayed alongside as I climbed the stairs to our room, trying to be helpful and fussing around like a broody hen, and I kept quiet.

I should have known the day before that she was in danger, I thought, should have dragged her down to the river and scrubbed her good, then bought her some clothes and sent her back to her people.

What people? I thought bitterly. She was probably the last of them. Murdered, mutilated, and left for the buzzards.

In the hotel room I looked at myself in the bureau mirror and saw a bony hound-dog face. On top of that rode a thick white bandage that made me look like Old Mother Hubbard with an empty cupboard.

"That'll have to go," I said, sitting down on my cot and leaning back against the wall.

"Not yet," Skofe said. "Rest easy. I'll be back in a minute."

"Where you goin'?" I asked, just to be asking.

"I'm going to go get a pail of beer for you. Beer's the best brain medicine ever invented."

"I don't need it," I said. "You go ahead and drink my share."

"You're sure?" he asked, standing in the doorway.

"I'll see you later, Skofe," I said, lying back and easing my head onto the pillow.

"That's the way," he said. "When you wake up we'll get down to business."

"Got to hurry some, I'm thinkin'," I said drowsily, and I closed my eyes, so sick of the world I couldn't fake another kind word.

The vision of the rimrock-enclosed park in northern Colorado Territory lifted out of the past and filled my mind. A swift-running stream ran through the pines and the deep grass. Deer, elk, and buffalo came there in their seasons, and the Arapahoe kept a permanent camp there where they could always return from their nomadic hunting trips, bearing enough meat and hides to sustain them through a snowed-in winter.

No more than thirty lodges; they were compact and complete in their life, and they could have killed me when I rode in with my pack horses and trapping gear. I was big, strong, wild, and, like most Texans, so confident that I felt I was invulnerable. I should never have survived that trip into Arapahoe country.

I'd tried mining around Denver, but grubbing in the mud didn't suit my free style. Somewhere I heard of the Valley of Many Mink, and I outfitted in Creede and pushed off into Indian Territory.

Crazy, or—if you're charitable—call it foolhardy. Whatever it was, I bet the aces of youth and strength and quickness against whatever destroyer lay out there in the mountains and parks.

I came in late in the summer, about this time of year when the birch leaves were quaking, sending gold pieces fluttering away on the northern wind, and

I blundered right into the middle of the camp before I even knew it.

There was no backing out once they'd seen me. The warriors had just returned from their regular summer horse-stealing raids and were still hot enough to kill a stranger without reason.

I'd kept them out of my packs but gave them a sack of salt and some bars of black cane sugar, and that slowed 'em down enough so we could make some sign talk.

"What do you want?" an old man had signed at me.

"I want to stay here," I signed back.

The biggest and most hotheaded of the warriors jumped up, yelled something, and pulled his knife.

It beat having to fight the whole camp.

I finally dislocated his right elbow. He cooled off some after I showed them how to pull it back into place again.

Afterward I shared out the trade beads and looking glasses and such and settled in. I thought it was interesting that once they'd decided not to kill me, they just figured I was there, the same as them.

I was building a lean-to of lodge-pole pines that I meant to cover with my tarpaulin when she came up the creek into my camp.

She looked over the boxy framework and shook her head. It wouldn't do. It must be a tepee or I would freeze.

She was a tall, slim girl of maybe fourteen years. She wore a buckskin sheath decorated with beads and fringes. Her thick hair, glossy blue-black, was parted in the middle and hung down in braids to her slender waist.

In that noble age of chivalry I had decided even before I left Texas that I would never take advantage of any Indian maiden, no matter how powerful the temptation. My job was to make a fortune by hard work and sacrifice, then return to Texas and raise cows.

How could I have been such a simpleton?

"No." I shook my head and made signs that I liked my lean-to.

I stretched my tarp over the poles, and she commenced bringing pine needles to cover the floor.

I didn't know how to tell her that I was a chivalrous knight from Texas.

But I didn't buy her. I didn't offer her any beads or trade goods, nothing. I pretended she wasn't there.

She would not eat with me but stood by my side watching.

Her eyes were great dark almond shapes tilted above her cheekbones. Her skin was fine-grained, shining fresh and golden. Her face was oval, her nose straight, her mouth wide, her lips full, but it was the tilted eyes that could look so strong and wistful at the same time that made a coward out of me.

Towards dark she went into my lean-to and sat down.

I grabbed a blanket and headed for the tall timber.

She was still sitting there next morning when I returned. She still had that power and tender wistfulness in those strange eyes. She looked up at me and smiled like she was glad to see the grizzlies hadn't ate me during the night.

It was that way for three days and nights, with her bringing me my food and waiting on me, and me disappearing into the bosk at dark time. She always had the prettiest smile when I turned up in the morning, and as time went by I'd ask her to help me with some small thing, and sometimes our hands would touch.

She brought a buffalo robe and covered the pine-needle mattress with it, hair-up, but she persisted in saying the lean-to was no good for this place.

Her father came over one day, looked the camp over, and shook his head. Then he scolded her and took her back to the tepee.

I was busy sorting out my traps and scouting the long valley for beaver and mink sign, but I missed her cheerful smile and tilted, wistful eyes.

I visited the camp and saw how the warriors, bored with lying around camp, abused their wives, beating and kicking them. And I could see why Spring naturally liked living with me more than with one of them.

Then I was feeling sorry for her and all the other women who not only did all the work but were beaten and kicked for no reason.

She showed up one mellow autumn afternoon, her manner very serious and straightforward. She made me understand that she would have to marry that big, crazy son of a bitch I'd fought with unless I would give her father one of the old muskets I'd brought along in my trade goods.

There was no wishy-washy about her. It was yes or no.

I looked into those great tilted eyes and visualized that big bastard kicking her in the rump, and I drew the musket out of my pack and walked with her to her father's tepee.

He took the musket, tried the hammer, and asked for powder and lead. I nodded, and he went back into his tepee, saying nothing more. When we walked back to my lean-to she stayed behind me.

At camp I tried to tell her I'd traded the musket so that she needn't marry anyone if she didn't want to. She was sad. Why didn't I want to marry her? she asked, her eyes no longer looking into mine but cast down in shame.

She explained that if I didn't accept her as my woman, she would be disgraced and punished.

I sat down on the buffalo robe that late afternoon and listened to the lazy buzzing of bees and the quacking of ducks overhead beating their way south. I smelled the golden autumn spices and felt the warmth of the late sun, and I laughed.

She'd boxed in the gallant white knight. The wings of chivalry were pinned by a fourteen-year-old Arapahoe maiden. The Texas do-gooder could not achieve sainthood against the witchcraft of a child.

Her golden body shone with the radiance of youth and passion. Her shoulders were wide, and her breasts jutted out firm as apples, and yet soft as beaver felt to my touch. Her waist was slim and hard, and her muscular hips flared out to establish her long, graceful legs. She was a peach ripened on the tree, as sweet and luscious as anything could be, and she picked herself from that tree and gave herself to me.

I touched her, and she touched me. I kissed her, and she returned the kiss. I tasted her body through the night, and she returned my gift. My rough passion brought out her own womanly emotions and physical responses. She was a virgin, but she needed no lessons in love. Her body was as natural as the river and the big trout and the willows weaving in the evening.

In the morning the Texas Galahad felt ten feet tall and ready to take on the real world. She made a man out of me, made me feel virile and honorable and powerful, and she took nothing back except the goodness in my heart.

She was ready when the weight of the first snow broke through the top of the lean-to. She had the poles and robes cached nearby, and with some help from our friends we were living in a warm tepee before nightfall.

About November she thought she was pregnant and was close to tears with joy.

In February a prospector came through from Denver with news that Lincoln was elected, and that Texas had seceded from the Union. He said there would be a war between the states within a few months, and Texas was calling for volunteers.

Call me a fool, call old Sam a rotten son of a bitch,

but I felt obliged to go. I told her it would be over in a few months and I'd be right back. I left my pelts and traps with her and saw that her family would help her while I was gone.

I did my best. Good old fool Sam did his rotten best.

Five years later I could come back to the Valley of Many Mink even though it was already history that the Colorado Volunteer Militia had massacred all the men, women, and children of that Arapahoe camp in 1864 under a white flag of truce.

I came back because I said I'd come back, and I found nothing left to show that some nice people had lived there once. . . .

I groaned as the vision of that tall, lithe girl flooded up through my mind, golden, radiant, her great brown eyes tilted up at the corners. . . .

I heard steps in the hall and tried to rub the traces of agony off my face. When Skofer came in the door I sat up and looked at the floor so he couldn't see my eyes.

"How're you a-doin', Sam?" he cackled with beery good humor. "Ready to tree the town?"

"Not quite. I'm more interested in catchin' that skunk that's guttin' out the squaws."

"Didn't the commander say to stay out of that sorry business?"

"I'm buyin' in."

"There's no way you can win," Skofer protested. "There's just too many folks hate Injuns to pick one out of the bunch."

"Whoever's doin' it has got some special grudge, some extra particular reason. I'll bet I can whittle it down to no more'n half a dozen hombres."

"If you say so," Skofer said doubtfully. "'Course, you could start with Liver Eater Maric. His grudge is no secret."

"I'd put in Tom Custer, but I don't think he was here last night," I said. "How about Rafe Egan?"

"Egan once made his livin' sellin' scalps. Sure, I'd put him on the list."

"That ex–Major Fred Hawes?"

"Cashiered for cowardice at Pony Creek." Skofe nodded. "He's big enough and hates redskins more'n most."

"I'm goin' to leave out the regular cattlemen," I said. "None of them have been here long enough."

"How about Doc Schreich?"

"Why?"

"He's been here a year or two."

"It's somebody more like Moon Gould, that big-mouthed scout," I said.

Skofer frowned. "Anyone else?"

"That baron is a wild card," I said. "I can't see him gettin' blood on his hands, but he's passin' strange. You got any more?"

"There's one you haven't met. Name of Calvin Hastings. He's some kind of a journalist who works for the baron."

"What's he done?"

"Nothing much, just spouting off down at the Elephant about the Indians ought to be exterminated

—mercifully, but exterminated—in the name of progress."

"I'll talk to him. Any more?"

"We should add in Fred Keogh," Skofer said. "I heard how his sister was kidnapped by the Comanches and never seen again."

— 5 —

MAKING LISTS AND GUESSING GAMES WASN'T GETTING the job done. I walked the floor, racking my still-thumping brain for a better idea, while Skofer looked out the window at the bustling street below.

"Skofer, so far no one has noticed us together except Keogh and Doc Shreich," I said. "Maybe we better keep it that way."

An idea buzzed around in the back of my head like a bee looking for a flower.

Part of the idea was the strange fact that Skofer, so long as he keeps halfway sober, is almost invisible in a bunch of people.

"Where did you go when you and Wagon Tongue Nellie were hootin' and hurrawin'?"

"It was a very tender and solemn evening." Skofer sounded offended. "We spent the entire evening in her rooms playing whist."

"I'm thinkin' on somethin'," I said. "You go ahead and get your horse. I'll meet you over at the river camp."

He stared at me, shook his head doubtfully, and muttered, "I reckon you do mean to fix it. . . ."

I gave him a few minutes' head start and tried to worry out what was bothering me. Something about the baron and Rafe Egan, or maybe it was the banker Kennefik. I put on my hat and considered having the harness maker make me a kind of helmet of bull's hide that would fit inside and protect my thinker.

The steeldust, with his neck bowed and his ears pricked up, trotted down Front Street to the fork and crossed the tracks. Nauchtown was quiet as feathers in a sack. Around at the riverbank I found Skofe talking to an old squaw.

The squaw was pointing at a cottonwood tree down the slope as I dismounted.

"They wanted to put her up on a scaffold in the tree," Skofer said, "but the whites said she had to be buried."

"Where was Satin Dancer killed?" I asked the old squaw, putting a quarter in her withered hand.

The squaw pointed at a firepit made of three rocks. "Her camp."

There was nothing of hers left except a few empty bottles.

"No blood?" I asked.

She put her finger to the nape of her neck and said, "Stab. Heap quick."

Count your blessings, I thought. It was quick instead of slow. It was clean instead of blood slopping all over the place. It was quiet instead of flopping around like a chicken with its head chopped off. But don't call it merciful.

"No one heard anything?"

She lifted a bottle, made a toothless, sardonic smile, and said, "Heap sleep."

The others were close by but so drugged down by the distillate they were helpless. A man could kill one every night and they wouldn't change a thing.

I went over to the new mound of earth by the cottonwood. The soil was rich, deep silt, easy to dig. She was enclosed, she was safe, she was gone from the time we kept.

Thanks to the Colorado Volunteers, a village of peaceful hunters was gone from the Valley of Many Mink, and a farmer had replaced them. It wasn't the farmer's fault. It was the fault of the Great White Father in Washington. It was the fault of every greedy land-grabber in America, and every corrupt politician who shared in the plunder and pillage.

"Be nice if the killer would drop something, like a watch with his name engraved on the back," Skofer said.

"Be nice." I nodded. "But this man is smart as a wolverine."

"The quiet kind." Skofer nodded.

"Likes to set back and watch the antics of kangaroo courts and admire his work," I muttered. "Keepin' quiet is part of his system."

"Makes it harder," Skofer said. "He could be anybody."

"No. He's got to be one of those on our list. Otherwise he'd be killin' whites, too."

"What are we doing about the Terrazas cows?" Skofe changed the subject. "Commander's going to be some disturbed we lose them."

"There's time."

"Where are they?"

"I don't know, but they haven't been shipped yet. And that's where you come in. From now on you don't know me."

"What deviltry are you fixing up for me now, Sam?" Skofer squawked like I'd jabbed him with a pitchfork.

I told him what I wanted him to do and gave him five double eagles.

"If you spend that on Wagon Tongue Nellie, I'm goin' to send you over to Doc for lower glandular surgery," I warned him.

After he'd gone I looked over the area again.

The old toothless squaw drifted over and crooned, "Fuckee two bits?" Gray lice crawled around the cocklebburs in her hair.

I shook my head and climbed aboard the steeldust.

I wondered if my anger and disgust reflected the moral training of my childhood or whether it came from the fear that all Americans, including me, would say "fuckee two bits" if our people were decimated, our rituals destroyed, and our homeland taken. Would we sell the remnants of our pride to the oppressor for a promise of security? Would we welcome a drug to blot out the horror of degradation? Oh, no, not Sam Benbow. Good Sam would fight to the death for his independence. Sure. Probably. Maybe. But suppose they wore you down slow so you couldn't fight back? What do you think, Sam, really?

Too much. My head was aching again.

I followed the trail back toward town, passing through Nauchtown without even seeing the flimsy cribs, when I noticed the single two-story house with the sign Polly's Palace.

Looked interesting. Somebody had a sense of humor.

The hitch rail was empty. It was early, but someone should have been up, I thought. Anyway there was no sign that said open or closed.

I stomped on the little front porch to get the mud off my boots and pushed open the door into the hall. Team bells jingled.

I smelled fresh coffee and bacon frying, and a tall, lanky black lady came out of a room to the rear and said, poker-faced, her eyes keen and appraising, "You early or late, mister. I'm just the maid. What you want?"

"Cup of coffee'd be fine." I smiled.

"That's easy." She showed her perfect white teeth. "Trying to wake up one of my ladies before noon is not so easy."

She led me back into the kitchen, where a pine drop-leaf table and four simple ladder-back chairs occupied the side near the back door.

On a cast-iron range an enamel coffee pot gave off a fine, rich aroma, and a black iron skillet was crowded with sizzling sliced bacon.

"Care for a late breakfast?" she asked. "Cost you four bits."

"Fine." I said, and I told her my name.

"I'm Clarissa." She made the looping quick smile again, and just that was enough to chase out the moldy mourning I'd felt earlier. She poured my coffee and asked doubtfully, "You just come for breakfast?"

"Partly," I said. "I wanted to talk to someone. Polly, I guess."

"Madame Polly is sleepin'," Clarissa said. "About six o'clock this afternoon she come down and become queen of Dodge."

She brought me a plate full of bacon and basted eggs, and another plate of corn bread and butter. Then she poured herself a cup of coffee and said, "Mind if I set with you?"

"Sit down, Clarissa." I stood and pulled a chair out for her.

"My, ain't you the gallant knight of the prairie," she said with a chuckle, her laughter like chocolate syrup.

"Pretty busy last night?" I asked between bites.

"We busy every night." Clarissa nodded. "Lotsa money here. Madame Polly all set to add on an annex for the overflow."

"Hombres stay all night?"

"Some." She nodded.

"Know their names?"

"You some kind of police?" Her dark eyes narrowed.

"Not that kind, Clarissa. I'm curious about the murders down at the river camp. That's not so far away it wouldn't worry you some, too."

"I have had dreams about that man with his knife slicin' a T in my belly and gatherin' up my—"

"When he runs out of squaws, where do you think he'll go next?"

"I know that, I know!" she exclaimed. "What names you want?"

"Just the men who stayed all night."

"There was that man they call the baron. He with Miss Leslie. There was his friend, the spunky little gent . . ."

"Hastings. Calvin Hastings?"

"That one." She nodded. "And the banker man, but he didn't hold out all night," she said, frowning, trying to remember. "I guess that's all. The rest were just drummers and crazy cowboys, in and out."

I scrubbed a chunk of corn bread across my plate and pushed the empty plate aside.

"Fred Keogh ever stay the night?"

"He been here," Clarissa said. "I don't remember how long he stay."

"Ever look out on the trail toward the river camp at night?" I tried my last long-shot question.

"Sometimes. When I'm tired—but I don't mean to. I don't want to see nothin'!"

"But did you ever see anything unusual?"

"What's unusual?" she asked, rolling her eyes. "Is a man walkin' along in the early mornin' with a box on his shoulder unusual?"

"I'd think so. Can you describe him?"

"No. I just seen the outline in the moonlight. Middle-sized. Wore a big black hat. Looked like old mister rawhaid bloody bones comin' to carry me away. I run upstairs and hid under my bed!"

"You didn't see his hands?"

"No, honest, I didn't see nothin' except that man in black, wearin' a big black hat, carryin' a shiny box on his shoulder."

"Thanks, Clarissa." I left a silver dollar on the table.

"If you ain't the law, why you doin' this?" she asked suddenly.

"Don't you know?"

"Sure I know." She flashed her beautiful smile. "I had it right the first time. You the gallant knight of the prairie."

"Not likely," I said, then I went out to the steeldust and rode back up the north bank of the river westerly.

Once I was clear of the godforsaken outcasts the firm, rich prairie opened up and revealed the vast expanse of grasslands slowly rising toward the Rockies three hundred miles away.

We called it the Big Pasture.

The first herd I met was on the move toward Dodge. Strung out in a line a mile long and being pressed along by half a dozen riders on either side, the herd came on at a steady walk. I quickly veered off to the left point, where the ramrod ought to be, and met a slim cowboy about my age.

"Mornin'," he said, his eyes scanning the ground ahead.

"Brand inspector," I said. "These all Double-Mill Irons?"

"Yes, sir," the ramrod said.

"John Slaughter's?"

"That's right. From down near Abilene."

"I'm from over by Austin," I said. "I'm lookin' for some cows with a fancy Mexican brand and a right ear underslope."

"Don't know it," the ramrod said. "Never seen it."

"Good luck," I said, touching my hat brim, and I rode clear of the herd and the cloud of dust they were raising.

A couple miles to the north I saw a trace of dust in the air and single-footed the steeldust over that way.

The herd was spread out, grazing northward but not being driven. Four cowhands spaced evenly around the herd sat their saddles on ponies that didn't move. The riders were just putting in time guarding the herd in case of trouble that might come from anywhere.

They were fat-backed steers with wide horns, and they were branded with Print Olive's Bar O. Their right ears were marked with a steeplefork, exactly as they should have been.

In camp their chuckwagon was set up, and half a dozen punchers lazed around mending tack, cleaning up, or snoozing in the shade.

Print Olive was staying in Dodge while his herd waited its turn. The foreman, a bandy-legged little ball of fire named Shorty Diggs, said he was in no hurry to drive his cattle into the railroad pens.

"They're makin' money for the brand every time they grab a bite of this grass," he said. "We'll take it slow."

No, he hadn't seen a fancy Mexican brand or the Terrazas earmark, but he'd heard of the spread.

"They say it's near as big as Texas," he said with a sort of awe.

"Can't be." I smiled. "There ain't nothin' that big."

I ate chuck with them and, following Shorty Diggs's directions, rode southwesterly to find the Nelson Story herd, with his initials on the butt of every cow and the left split ear.

Story, an old man who'd come up the trail in a buckboard, knew nothing of the Terrazas, but he directed me due west to a waiting herd belonging to some kind of foreigner named Baron something or other.

It was a good-size herd of about three thousand head, all busy eating and putting on tallow that would never have happened in the spiny, arid land of southwest Texas. It was said that cattle from that area would double their weight just walking up to the trail because of the richness of the grass.

The usual guards loafed around the perimeter of

the herd, and I saw that the Frying Pan brand was bigger than I'd expected, and the grubbed right ears couldn't be more grubbed because they were cut off close to the skull.

I, for one, had been trying for a couple of years to make that mark illegal within our Cattlemen's Association, because it eliminated any mark someone else might have put there first. So it really didn't mean a mark of ownership; it just meant you could identify a herd of cattle very quickly.

Humorous Mexican vaqueros called it *"Quedo?"* meaning "What's left?"

As for the Frying Pan , it was of such a shape and size that it could be used to obliterate any brand underneath it, the same as the Iron Pot or the spider . They just weren't a hundred percent honest. There was always a lack of confidence in cattlemen who used that type of blot brand.

Still, those men were unruly and powerful, and you could get yourself killed awfully quick just by shaking your head doubtfully about such a brand.

Of course, the baron wasn't in camp, but his ramrod, Rafe Egan, was.

They'd set up camp next to the river in a grove of black walnuts where the living was easy after several months coming up the trail.

I noticed the off-duty riders were more interested in cleaning and oiling their weapons than their saddles or chaps or saddle wallets.

They seemed cut from different cloth, too—drovers, all right, but without much of a smile or horseplay. Still, I knew the drive could be hellish if things went wrong, and it took the smile out of plenty of foolish cowboys.

Rafe Egan was dealing stud poker to two punchers sitting on blankets in the shade. The cards were so old the pictures were half worn off, and their edges looked like saw teeth where the players had tried to mark them with their fingernails.

Egan tossed down a queen of hearts face up to the man on his left and said, "Queen bets."

The player tossed out three beans. Egan looked up at me, waited a long moment to show his contempt, then said, "Light down and set. Grub's gone, but we're heavy on water."

The players snickered and went on with their game.

"I'm just passin' through," I said, not shifting in the saddle. "No offense, but did you boys bring your herd up from around San Angelo?"

"You could say that," Rafe Egan sneered. "You interested in buyin' 'em?"

"Not exactly," I said. "I'm just lookin' for a couple friends comin' up the trail from Hudspeth County."

"If you're talkin' about El Paso, why don't you just say so?" Egan said, getting to his feet slowly, his thin hatchet face fixed, his little eyes hidden behind long, sunburned white eyelashes.

I held up one hand palm forward. "Sometimes folks are a little scratchy when a stranger mentions that town, and I'm not lookin' for trouble, just a couple of peelers I rode with once."

"I seen you in town, didn't I?" Egan asked, wrinkling his narrow forehead to remember. "You wasn't very anxious to help us hang that fat Injun."

"That's true," I said. "I was thinkin' he didn't need to be hung."

"Was he guilty or not?" Egan challenged me.

"Not hardly. Another squaw was killed in the same way just a few hours later."

"But you didn't know any different before," Egan fired back, some salty.

"Nobody did for sure. I reckon I'll mosey along."

"You don't mosey till I'm finished," he snarled, drawing his Colt forty-four. "I'm damned if you do!"

I wondered if I was going to have to kill him.

"Mister, I come here peaceable. You may think you are the big he-boar of the purple prairie, but you are not."

"Who the hell are you?" he gritted out, lowering the revolver so that it pointed more toward the ground than me.

"My name's Sam Benbow," I said, setting back in the saddle so that the steeldust stepped back. "My friends are named John Wesley Hardin and Clayton Allison."

"How come you like to kiss the goddamned Injuns' ass?" he sneered, too puffed up with his own blood lust to listen to sensible talk.

The poker players were on their feet, stepping back to catch me in a crossfire if it came to a fight, and I kicked myself for speaking my mind. Getting old and scratchy myself. Somebody insults you, you take it serious instead of thinking about living to fight another day when the odds are more even.

"You didn't answer me," Egan said slowly. "I'm askin' are you for the redskins or the white?"

"I'm for peace and plenty for everybody," I said, keeping the five men in my vision. They were all raspy and ready, like they hadn't had any fun since maybe they backshot the Terrazas vaqueros some months ago.

"Why don't somebody just top him off that bronc so's we can flog his ass with a wet rope?" One of the card players grinned with half of his face, his buck teeth mottled brown and yellow.

"Drag the son of a bitch," another said.

"Be careful, boys." Egan grinned thinly. "He looks a little mossy and fat, but he's still got his stinger."

"It's about time you started thinkin' on that," I said.

Times like these, my emotions and my simple thoughts retire to a little box somewhere in my upper backbone. I start feeling real comfortable, and my muscles feel connected directly into the backs of my eyeballs.

When it gets to the point there's only one way to save your neck, survival overrides all the other foolishness, and I just set back and watch, knowing if it doesn't come out the way I think it will, that'll be the end of old Sam; but I don't worry overly because the other jasper is so fired up, his whole body is tensed tight while he's trying to think up different ways of killing me. I'm not that way. I know I'm going to stop him.

I leaned back in the saddle again, and the steeldust backed up another couple steps.

Would I kill all five of them? I didn't know and didn't worry about it. I watched Egan. Either he'd start it and die, or he wouldn't and live.

"Better for you if you hold down your wolf and I ride off," I said softly.

"You said I wasn't the big he-boar of the prairie," Egan said tightly. "If I'm not, who is?"

"I am," I said in the same quiet, unthreatening voice.

"Well, I'll be go to hell!" Egan forced a laugh. "I never even heard of a gunfighter named Benbow. You, boys?"

"Looks to me like if you bend him over, he'd be pretty good," the bucktoothed one crowed.

Egan moved so that the steeldust's neck and head were in between him and me, and I kneed the good horse a shade to the left.

"I got a feelin' you're a Pinkerton or a Texas Ranger," Egan said carefully. "Nobody rides into a cattle camp and starts bein' nosy."

"I stopped in at three other cattle camps earlier, and nobody worried about it."

"What's that supposed to mean?" Egan snarled back, hot again, taking a step forward.

"The Good Book says the guilty flee when no man pursueth," I said, moving the steeldust back a step.

"Guilty!" he yelled, and his right hand lifted the gun. Without a guiding thought my spurs touched the steeldust, and he leapt forward.

Egan had to jump aside, and as his gun came up again I shot him right through the wedge of his nose, a kill shot. Then the steeldust whirled, and my bullet smashed through the smart aleck's buck teeth, leaving a surprised look on the rest of his face.

A shot roared off to my left that burned by my upper left arm.

I turned to take him, too, but they'd scattered into the walnut grove.

After a quick quarter mile I slowed the steeldust down, and my thinker took over.

— 6 —

WHEN THE TWO-FIFTEEN FROM ELLSWORTH AND points east arrived, the dogs barked, housewives downwind gathered in their sheets from the clotheslines, and the usual number of unemployed cowboys strolled down to the depot, hoping to see something that would enliven the day.

The brass-trimmed engine was an American 4-4-0 followed by the wooden mail and baggage car, with two day coaches and a caboose.

The conductor stood by to help the female passengers with babies down the steps while the engineer oiled the driving wheels with a long-spouted oilcan and brakemen prowled around either end of the train pretending to be busy.

Two families of immigrants got off. From the cut of

their drab clothes and the terrorized look on their faces, they were probably coming directly from the Baltic coast.

Three drummers wearing bright striped or checked suits and carrying large leather cases of sample goods got off, and that seemed to be the whole ten-cents-a-mile supercargo. The unemployed spectators were disappointed. The conductor bent down to pick up his footstool and was ready to signal the engineer when on the vestibule landing a languid, apple-cheeked dandy appeared.

A small, thin, foppish-looking gentleman, he wore a pearl-gray frock coat, pin-striped trousers, and a ruffled white shirt with a casual four-in-hand black tie. A gray plug hat trimmed with silk ribbon added something to his small stature.

He was clean-shaven except for a silvery sweeping mustache, and on his nose was perched a pince-nez, the latest style in spectacles.

To give him credit, he did not look anything like the Skofer Haavik who'd ridden easterly the day before.

A silver-mounted cane hung over his left wrist as he dawdled at the top of the steps, giving everyone a free look.

"Don't that beat all!" breathed a wide-eyed, whiskery cowboy.

"Man in all his glory," murmured his companion.

Leisurely stepping down to the footstool, and permitting the conductor to take his elbow and steady his step, the dude murmured to the conductor, "Please send my luggage to the Astor House," and he pressed a silver dollar into the conductor's hand.

"Yessir." The conductor nodded, saluting, and he hurried off to give the baggage man the orders.

From out of the crowd came Baron Alexis Nabokov, Calvin Hastings, and Kennefik, the rotund banker.

The dynamic Hastings took the lead, introducing himself first and then his companions.

"Your letter of credit arrived this morning by telegraph, Mr. Pierpont"—Kennefik beamed—"and it seems in perfect order."

"It had better be, or heads will roll in New York!" Skofer Pierpont replied sternly.

"Come along, we'll show you around," Hastings said.

"Yes, I would like to see a real cowboy, and perhaps an Indian, if there are any left."

"We'll show you plenty of cowboys, but I'm afraid the Indians are down in the Five Nations," Baron Nabokov said, eyeing the New York dude as if he reminded him of someone else.

"Should I buy a gun?" Skofer Pierpont asked as they strolled down the boardwalk.

"I don't think it will be necessary." The baron smiled. "We'll look after you."

"It's good to have someone to count on," Skofer Pierpont drawled languidly. "I'd not like to have to take my cane to some western ruffian mistreating a horse."

"Have you read the prospectus on the Great Western Meat Products Company?" Hastings asked as they went into Delmonico's.

What could go wrong? I wondered. What had I overlooked?

If Skofer could stay alert and sober, he should have no problems.

I went back to the depot, and in the telegraph office I asked the pale tan-haired wireman for any messages.

"One just in," he said, getting up from his key and looking through a small stack of telegrams. He wore black wristbands that extended on up his lanky arms. It looked like he was elbow-deep in mourning.

"Charges paid," he said, handing over a sheet of yellow paper on which was block-printed: NEED MORE TIME FOR ENGRAVING GOLD WATCH. Frasier.

Baron Nabokov was still a mystery man. The commander would eventually uncover whatever needed uncovering, but there wasn't much time. With Rafe Egan dead the baron would likely want to sell the herd quickly.

He had held back driving the herd into the railroad pens because there it was make or break. There could be an accident. Someone might talk. There might easily be sharp-eyed inspectors, and there could be decoy cattle marked with silver coins hidden under their hides that would bring down the whole scheme. Rustling was a dangerous business all the way to market.

I went on over to the shipping office by the pens

and asked the clerk if any new herds had been reported coming in.

He looked at the final page of his journal and nodded. "There's the Cherry brand that crossed the river last evening."

"I don't know that brand," I said.

"Supposed to be from down around Uvalde. Probably a mavericker setting himself up in business." The clerk smiled. "It's a blot brand."

I understood it then. The cherry would be a solid round burn, and it would have a curved line coming out of the right side of it to make the stem.

"Grubbed earmark?"

"No"—he looked at his book again—"this one has a full crop on the left."

"Not much difference. Who owns 'em?"

"Arnold Cherry," the clerk said.

I went on out to look at the penned Texas *cimarrones,* the meanest, trickiest animals known to man, including the grizzly. Their fighting skills were refined by the thorny thickets, the cactus, and the hot, arid land.

I admired them because they survived and weren't sneaky about it.

Maybe they wouldn't survive much longer, because they were being driven north in the millions now, and I doubted they could reproduce that fast.

What kind of an America would it be if the longhorn went the way of the buffalo?

I smelled a smoky, noxious odor, felt a tug at my sleeve, and heard a high-pitched voice. "Mister . . ."

I turned and saw the toothless, barefoot squaw

looking up at me through her long, matted hair. She motioned for me to come along with her, and we worked around the pens to the river camp, a place I didn't want to return to so soon.

I was afraid she was going to show me another gutted-out squaw, but she led me on through the camp, with its scattered lumps of derelicts huddled here and there, crying out hopelessly, "Money . . . money . . ." when they saw me passing through.

She led me down a bank to a wooden area next to the river, then made her way through the trees in a roundy-bouty way until we were at the water's edge.

The mud bank had a groove in it that she explained by making paddling signs. A canoe or boat had come ashore in the night.

Two sets of footprints made a curved trail around the trees and up the bank toward the Indian camp. Sometime later the pair from the boat had returned. I thought their returning boot prints were set deeper in the silt, as if they were carrying a load.

"Who are they?" I asked.

She shrugged her shoulders, then bowed and patted her right shoulder. A man carrying something on his right shoulder.

I wondered if it was a tin box, but she couldn't tell me.

I looked across the wide, shallow river, thinking maybe the boat had come over from the other side.

Yet no one had been killed in camp last night.

"Thank you," I said, giving her a silver quarter. "What is your name?"

"Mary." She grinned, then repeated by rote what some joker had taught her. "Me Mary Mother of God."

That kind of wit sent my spirit down in a sickening spiral. I wanted to get away from that place and those people.

I'd have to check both sides of the riverbank for miles to find the boat, and there wasn't time. The cattle were moving through the pens just as fast as the cattle cars could carry them east. The Frying Pan would be moving into the shipping pens, and when it left, it wasn't coming back.

There was nothing I could do about it until I had authority from the commander to arrest the baron and impound the herd for a detailed inspection, which might show that a cowboy had been careless with his branding iron and hadn't covered all the Terrazas brand, or a cow had been missed in the over-branding and still carried its unblotted mark.

I left Mary at the camp, worked my way through the alleys and gates of the cow pens to the railroad tracks, and crossed over to Front Street. Without looking at the sun I knew it was time for a drink.

In the New Elephant I ordered Tennessee whiskey. Tasting it first, I figured it wouldn't dissolve my innards and might do something to blow the gloom out of the back of my head. I finished the glass and then ordered a glass of beer.

Maric left the table where he'd been playing solitaire and moved heavily my way. I noticed a glint of white showing in his beard. Silver tip. Getting old. Not the only one, either.

I wondered how a trapper made a living down in the middle of the Big Pasture where there wasn't enough valuable pelts to keep a man in beans.

He ordered a glass of the clear but took his time drinking it. Something on his mind.

"No offense," he said, turning toward me. "I'm lookin' for a grubstake partner. It ain't no game to rob you of your money, it's the pure quill."

"What's the offer?" I asked.

"Silver. It's way to hell and gone from here, but it ain't so high up you can't get to it in winter."

"You got it staked yet?"

"No. I don't know how big it is. I was running my lines when I fell and broke my leg. Had to crawl out for help."

"All the way to Dodge?"

"Hell, there ain't nothin' in Dodge except cows," he said disgustedly. "No, I made it into Denver until I could walk and then went back to Missouri to look up a man I knew that had money. He was dead. There was no money. I had enough left to buy a ticket to here. Now I'm afoot, the purse is empty, and I'm still four hundred miles from a mountain of money."

His sun-cured forehead was lined deeply with grooves that hooked down his temples and framed his gunsight eyes.

"I thought you were a trapper."

"I was, and we took many a pack train of furs out of the Bitteroots, and the Kamispell, but don't you know an outdoors man can't keep ahold of money?"

"I guess you're thinkin' I'm an inside type." I smiled.

"I don't know." He smiled. "You look like an outsider, but you dress like an insider."

"Ever hear of the Valley of Many Mink?" I asked.

"Northern Colorado Park country." He nodded. "I never went in there myself. The Arapahoes were worse'n Blackfeet when it came to lettin' the white in."

"I trapped a winter there once a long time ago," I said, talking too much, but it was heavy on my mind, and I felt a sense of comradeship with the man who had tried to beat the devil the same as me.

"There's nothin' left there since the Militia burned it down," he said, aware now that I'd had to have gone in there before the massacre, and like most everyone else, I'd left some of my heart there when I left.

"Is that story about you true?" I changed the subject.

"About eatin' the Injun's liver?" He grinned. "No, not likely. Yarns get built up, you know, especially if you don't tear 'em down."

"How'd it start?" I asked, passing the time of day.

"There was a party of us trappers running from a band of Blackfeet as hard as we could go. They charged us, and I lost my partner, but I kilt one of the bucks. They was gettin' ready to run another charge on us, so I dragged that dead buck up on a high bank, opened him up, and made it look like I was eatin' his liver while I was warnin' 'em they were next. It scared the hell out of them so bad they left."

"I figured you didn't look like a man who could keep a hot liver down." I smiled.

"There's some good Injuns so long as they're in their place, but there's some that ought to be just eliminated for their own good," he said levelly.

"You mean the drunks over by the river."

"That's some of 'em," he said with a nod.

"Maybe you should have stayed with the ones up north," I said quietly.

"It was too hard bein' caught between them and the troopers. Got so nobody on either side trusted me. Those goddamned braves always figured I was against them. The older men understood my feelin's, but they died off, and the blue coats were grindin' us down. No way left but skedaddle." His voice had turned somber. He was telling something he'd carried for too long, and it had been eating at him like acid.

"A man only has one life"—he shook his head bitterly—"and everyone wants to run it for him."

"So you went to prospectin'," I said.

"Trappin' is good trainin' for prospectin'." He smiled, coming out of the dark mood that I understood very well. "It ain't near as much fun lookin' for rocks, but my scalp was some safer."

"Any ore samples?" I asked.

"Now you're jokin' me." He grinned, his eyes honest and unafraid. "You know I could show you samples of pure AG and tell you I had a map to right where I'd found 'em, but you ain't that empty between the ears."

"It's the usual approach, though." I nodded.

"But like I said, I ain't out to rob anybody with a tall story."

"I'm afraid you got the outdoor part of me right. Every time I make a little money, it flies away," I said.

"I'm not disappointed," he said. "A man takes the cards he's dealt and plays 'em best way he can. If I had her to do over again, I wouldn't change it much."

"Where are you stayin'?"

He hesitated a moment, looked off to nowhere, and said, "I'm campin' out yonder."

"Not at the river camp?" I said too fast.

"Mr. Benbow." He looked at me with disappointment in his eyes.

"No offense." I smiled. "When you said 'yonder' it just slipped out. Can I buy you a drink?"

"Thank you kindly, Mr. Benbow." He shook his head. "I've got to get down to the butcher shop and see if Spud's got any bones for my dog."

I couldn't tell if he was joking or not, and he didn't give me a clue nor say good-bye.

Hump-shouldered and with a hitch in his step, he walked out the door, a man who'd had the courage to meet the best of the old wilderness, and who thought some Indians were decent enough and some Indians ought to be eliminated for their own good.

If the war hadn't come along, I might have been the same man, worn down by the changing times.

"Do or die, we shall try," my daddy used to say after some freak natural disaster had destroyed his year's work. I'll still go along with that. All I want is a chance to try.

I went out onto the crowded boardwalk, walked over to the livery barn, and said hello to the old stableman, Pat Casey, whose right leg was so rigid from the hip down he had to swing it around in a half circle to take a step.

My steeldust seemed pleased to see me, and that cheers a man up. I borrowed a curry comb and brush, started on his silvery mane, and made a one-way conversation, which he didn't object to.

"Whoa—hold still. How're you feelin'? Gettin' enough to eat? Lookin' forward to a hard quarter run?"

To all this nonsense he wiggled his ears or scratched his chin on the feed box.

I found a hooked hoof knife, lifted the steeldust's front knee between my legs, and scraped the wet manure out of the frog, then smelled the hoof for rot, which stinks a lot worse than horse manure.

The rear hoof was dry and hard, too, and as I rubbed my hand over the steeldust's butt, telling him not to kick me, ex–Major Frederick Hawes came through the back door and blinked his wide-set eyes in the half light.

"That you, Red?" he asked.

His voice was thick and wet, and he smelled of high-proof clear. Long-waisted and stumpy-legged, he looked like a tall man who'd been cut off at the knees.

I stepped away from the gelding and said, "No, I'm Sam Benbow, horse brusher."

He backed up and said, "Sorry, I thought you were a trooper friend of mine. Couldn't see in the dark. . . ."

"I've seen you around, Major," I said neutrally. "You keep your horse here?"

"I don't have a horse," he said. "I have no need to ride anywhere."

"Some folks just ride for pleasure," I said, hoping I could get him talking. Maybe he'd make himself a prime murder suspect, or maybe he'd eliminate himself. Either way, I needed to know.

"I said I don't have a horse," he replied, his voice harsh and angry, his purple-veined nose and cheeks flushed. "It is irrelevant whether I ride for duty or for pleasure."

"You were in the Seventh Cavalry?"

"I was, sir, before the Custer boys came west to show us how to kill Indians."

"They seem to be pretty good at it once you get 'em started," I said. "'Course, they're not too particular how they go about doin' it."

"Indeed, the rules of war and the gentleman's code have been discarded by George and his brother. I pray the mills of the gods will grind them fine enough in my lifetime to justify my own beliefs."

"You against killin' Indians?" I asked, half smiling.

"If my duty is to kill Indians, I will do my duty," Hawes growled.

"How about just plain no-good Indians loafin' around, bein' drunk and disorderly?"

"These local beggars? I'd shoot every goddamned one of them if I had my way."

"They bother you some?"

"Just to see them is bothersome. They won't bathe, they won't work, they won't do anything except beg."

"I don't hold with beggin'," I said, "less'n of course you're starvin' or freezin' to death. Then you might break the rule."

"They beg for money to buy whiskey, not food," the ex-major snapped.

"Major, I'm not defendin' 'em. They are just what you say they are," I said. "I think it's some sorrowful it happened to them this way, but it's too late to do much about it."

"Sherman, Grant's insane comrade, said war is hell and proved it," Hawes growled. "I went into Atlanta with him, and we made those high-toned southern ladies beg like these squaws, except they spoke better English, and instead of sayin' 'fuckee two bits' they'd say, 'Major, would you'all care to come over to supper tonight and loan me five dollars?' It was all the same beggary," he recalled, chuckling.

"I always thought those southern ladies resisted the blue coats till the end." I smiled.

"War makes women beg. Any woman with hunger in the house will beg to do unspeakable things."

His eyes bulged and his lips pulled back, and his expression reminded me of a bulldog biting down on a steer's nose.

"I generally avoid that type of female," I said, thinking he was just as insane as General Sherman.

"You're from the south from the sound of your voice. Did you fight for that foolish cause?" He quieted down a little.

"Some." I shrugged. "Sometimes I run."

"Fire and steel make the man," he declared, like he'd said it a hundred times and it sounded good to him.

"I don't quite figure that," I said. "What does it mean?"

"I mean the fire of battle!" he snarled. "The steel of bayonet and sword!"

"You did a lot of fightin' on your way to Atlanta?"

"I was in the quartermaster corps. We were in the thick of it all the way."

"Shucks, Major." I grinned, brushing the steel-dust's back. "I heard them quartermasters got rich sellin' supplies to us barefoot southern boys."

"That is not true, sir." He stood on his toes and glared at me. "I don't know why I'm bothering with you."

"I figure it's because you and I both like horses," I said. "What do you do at night, dream of old battles or hope for a chance at more?"

"Mr. Benbow, I live in a shack in Nauchtown

because I lost a battle to the Cheyenne. I lost because my scout never returned. It's like losing your eyes. You don't know what's out there, and yet you can't back up for fear of being called cowardly. I guessed wrong. I backed off." His shoulders slumped.

"What happened to your scout, Major?" I asked quietly.

"A halfbreed. Scum. Thief. Gambler," he growled. "He's in town. I'll kill him someday."

"Do you have a family, Major?"

"My wife and children live in Maryland," he muttered, looking at the dirt floor.

"Why don't you go back and start all over again?"

"They are living with my wife's parents," he said. "I started with nothing when the war came. I have not yet finished with my campaign nor my war."

"Major," I said reasonably, "it's all over. Custer's on the way to Wyoming. He'll finish it along with Crook and Terry."

"God, I hope he meets them the way I did," Hawes said, his eyes glowing fervently. "I hope he loses his scouts. I hope he rides over the wrong hill."

"Sounds like you're for the Sioux."

"I'm for whatever force will destroy that arrogant coxcomb," Hawes muttered, "but Indians? No, their day is done. Best kill them like snakes, without mercy."

"All of 'em?"

"All of them!" he exclaimed, as if he'd suddenly

realized a great truth and found himself a holy mission. "They'll be begging forevermore. Gimme. Gimme. The bloody savages broke every sacred treaty and then came back to ask for more of this, more of that. Kill them like snakes, kill every last one of them, and wipe the slate clean!"

— 7 —

THE DAY HAD BEEN AS LONG AS THE AGE OF THE METHUselah of coons, and as I went up the steps to the veranda of the Drovers Inn the only thing on my weary mind was to stretch out on my cot and close my eyes. With any luck, sleep would come without any dreams.

Such an attitude can often be fatal.

I didn't pay any attention to the two men sitting in the rush-seated rocking chairs, passing the quiet hour when the locusts have just started to fiddle and the cowboys are yet to yodel. I nodded and started to open the door when the one on my right said, "Mr. Benbow?"

With my hand on the china doorknob I muttered, "That's me."

I heard the twin clicks of steel hammers being drawn back to full cock, and I raised my hands.

"Come along," the dry voice of the man on my right said, lifting my forty-four from its holster.

"Whereaway?" I asked as we went back down the steps to the boardwalk.

"Turn left," the dry voice said.

They kept just slightly behind me so that I couldn't see who they were or where to hit them if I felt suicidal.

"Nice evenin' for a walk," I volunteered, but neither of them was sociable.

Storefronts were shaded and doors padlocked for the day while the merchants sat in their easy chairs at home dandling youngsters on their knees or happily counting their day's receipts.

I decided I would rather fight than go into a dark alley with these hombres, and I tried to figure out a square-dance class where I called the steps.

Join hands and circle right . . .
And hold your holts and gone again . . .
Promenade and put her on a shelf,
If you want any more, you can call it yourself.

Before we reached the corner the dry voice directed me to turn right and knock on the door.

A small frame building, it fronted directly on the boardwalk, and in the gathering gloom I did as I was told.

In a moment the door was opened by the short,

fastidious, leonine Calvin Hastings, bubbling over with energy and know-how.

"Come in and sit down, Mr. Benbow." He opened the door wide and stepped aside. "We've been expecting you."

A milk-glass lamp with a frosted chimney lighted the low-ceilinged room, and as I entered I saw the massive, bald-headed Baron Nabokov sitting behind a broad desk.

The door closed as I took the chair opposite the baron, and Hastings found a seat off to my left.

"Thank you for coming, Mr. Benbow," Hastings said. "The baron has some business to discuss with you."

"Interesting invite," I said.

"You're a difficult man to . . . catch." Hastings smiled.

"Never mind," the baron said, leaning forward, his full black beard shining like he'd just oiled it. "You're here, and it will save time if I just ask—why did you kill my foreman?"

"Call it self-defense. He was a nervous man, worried a lot about his bravery. Fellow like that walks the razor's edge."

"What did he say to provoke you?"

"Baron, I wasn't provoked, I was just tryin' to get the hell out without showing my back."

"Words were said," he insisted.

"As I recall, he wanted to know why I wanted to kiss the goddamned Indians' ass."

"Forget the Indians. What was said about my

cattle?" Nabokov slammed the desktop with the flat of his hand.

"Wasn't anything said about cattle, yours or anybody else's. I was lookin' for a couple friends supposed to be comin' up the trail from Hudspeth County. Your foreman got after me on account of me bein' against the hangin'. That's the whole thing boiled down to poison."

The baron glanced at Hastings.

"What set Egan off?" Hastings asked.

"I quoted the Bible to him, and he went for his weapon."

"That's what Clint said." Hastings spoke to the baron in a quiet voice.

"He also said he thought you were some sort of undercover Pinkerton spy, and as I recall, Mr. McCoy said you were a stock detective?" The baron put it as a question.

"I was with a Cattlemen's Association for a while, but the pay wasn't enough for an old man to risk his neck for." I shook my head.

"There's no way we can check on that," the baron said heavily, his dark, deep-set eyes glowing like iron in a forge.

"I never asked you to prove who you are, nor him"—I jabbed a thumb at Hastings—"because I don't give a rat's ass who you are, so long as you leave me alone."

"Careful, Benbow," Hastings said sharply, getting to his feet, trying to make six foot four out of five foot four. "You are vulnerable."

"With two gunsels at my back and no weapon? I'd say that was plain as the wart on the old maid's nose." I smiled.

"Mr. Benbow, I am negotiating a business transaction that involves over a million dollars. I will not have you or any other stray adventurer interfering in this business. If you're a fiddle-footed cowboy, you don't count for anything. If you're a Pinkerton detective, you still don't count for anything. Understood?"

"I heard your brag," I said, "but it seems like you're interferin' in my business more'n I'm interferin' in yours."

"Americans! By God, I can't believe such insolence!" the baron exclaimed. "Get this fool out of here!"

I turned to the lean drink of water with the dry voice and said, "Give me my gun. If you're thinkin' of bendin' the barrel over my head, you better think twice, because I'm the ornery kind that carries a grudge."

"Give it to him, Snake." Hastings shook his head in exasperation.

"Hell, I was goin' to break his big mouth with it," Snake drawled, and he jammed the Colt back in my holster.

"Good night, gents," I said.

"Just a minute, Benbow." The baron tried again. "Who are these friends you're looking for?"

"Names are Clayton Allison and John Wesley Hardin," I said. "Those boys carry grudges, too."

Snake's eyes opened wide, and the side of his thin

mouth jerked. He was the only one who knew who I was talking about, and it made me wonder.

Outside, clumping down the dark boardwalk, I thanked my lucky stars that Snake hadn't pistol-whipped my poor head. It still wasn't right from the last time.

This time I made it up to my room without being stopped along the way. I kicked off my boots, unbuckled my belt, and lay my head on the pillow, but sleep wouldn't come. I stared into the darkness and wondered if I hadn't ought to be over by the river camp watching for the man with the shiny box on his shoulder. He seemed to kill whenever the mood hit him and not according to any schedule or phase of the moon. He could be over there right now cutting on Mary, Mother of God. . . .

Before I could settle my mind I heard a faint tapping on my door, like a man drumming his fingertips on a desk.

I stepped sock-footed onto the floor and eased over to the door.

"Quién está?" I whispered.

"Skofero," came the whispered reply, and I opened the door to let him in.

After lighting the lamp I looked over the smiling old peacock in his finery and nodded. "Good to see you, Skofero."

"Igualmente," he said with a grin.

"Been havin' a high old time?" I asked tiredly.

"I haven't hardly touched a drop," he protested, "but I got those boys' attention all right."

"What's the scheme?"

"Everything about it looks on the level." Skofer shook his head. "But I still don't believe it."

"What's wrong?"

"It's so big," he said, "like they want to take up about ten thousand acres west of here on either side of the river. They'll build their packing plant close to the railroad, but they'll have feeding pens behind the packing house where they'll fatten up the rangy longhorns into butterballs before they slaughter 'em."

"What do they feed 'em?"

"They're going to bring in a bunch of Russian farmers to grow the grain. The only thing they buy is ribby longhorns. They're even talking of putting a railroad straight south from Dodge to Texas, saving the longhorns a long walk."

"Makes sense." I nodded. "It just takes a lot of money and makin' sure nothin' goes wrong."

"I can't see what'd go wrong." Skofer shook his head.

"What about a flood or range fire, or a drought, or some kind of grain-lovin' bug that arrives just when things are lookin' good?"

"Those are natural disasters," Skofer said. "Nobody can do anything about them."

"Right," I agreed, "and what are they goin' to do for ice to keep the meat while it travels east?"

"I tell you, they got every rat hole covered," Skofer said enthusiastically. "They'll build a big ice plant with double walls full of sawdust, and they'll bring out a steam engine and other machinery that will make real ice. If I had any money, I'd sure load up on their stock. There's no way it can lose."

"The whole scheme is cool blue smoke up your backsides," I said. "They just figure to pack up the money and skedaddle with it."

"Why bother to steal it when they can double it in a couple years?" Skofer asked.

"It's the nature of the beast."

"That's not enough of a reason," Skofer objected.

"My guess is, then, that they're makin' their cost estimates too low. What they're talkin' about will take a hell of a lot more than a million dollars. Once someone figures they've cheated on their estimates, the whole thing will collapse."

"You mean it would take five million to build the complex?" he asked. "Not one?"

"Maybe ten," I said, "but they know they can't get the ten, so they lower the planned cost to make it look pretty as a little red heifer in a flower bed."

"How long you want me to play the fool?" Skofer asked, disappointed.

"I'd like to know how that Frying Pan herd fits in. Go along another day maybe, but don't get yourself killed."

He started for the door, then remembered something. "The squaws?"

"It's still too muddy. There's a man with a shiny box that goes by. There's two people in a rowboat that go through, but nobody knows who any of them are."

"You got somebody picked out?"

"One of 'em isn't Rafe Egan. He's dead. Custer's gone north. That lets him out."

Skofer extracted a leather-covered notebook and a pencil and flipped through the pages until he found a blank one.

"Let's be businesslike in this operation," he said reproachfully. "Give me all the names in your head."

"Start with Maric. Old-time squaw man, but the Blackfeet ran him out."

Skofer wrote down the name as I added, "Ex-Major Fred Hawes for losin' the battle."

Skofer wrote swiftly as I talked.

"There's Moon Gould, who hasn't been around lately but has a grudge, and then it gets a little thin."

"I want 'em all," Skofer said sharply.

"Well . . . I guess you could add on Doc Shreich. He wants 'em killed, but mercifully. There's Calvin Hastings; he wants 'em exterminated, all of 'em, and there's Fred Keogh, who might still have a grudge against the Comanches for stealin' his sister thirty years ago."

"That's a long list of possibles." Skofer closed the notebook and tapped the pencil against his foxy chin. "I can't see Hastings or Doc Shreich in it."

"They've all got their reasons," I said. "It just depends on how big the reason grows in the man's head."

"Couldn't be a woman?"

"Could, I reckon, if there's a crazy one stayin' over at Polly's Palace, but I'd say it's too gruesome for a female's mind."

"You left the baron out."

"He's got no reason that I can find, and he was with a sporter the night of the last killin'."

"I can ask a few questions about Hastings," Skofer said, "but the rest of them are on a different level than Skofer K. Pierpont."

"There's an Arickaree squaw over there named Mary that's been helpin'. She showed me the mark of the boat and the—"

A board creaked in the hall, and I shut my mouth.

We'd forgotten how thin the walls were, and we'd been talking in normal voices. I moved swiftly and silently across the room, drew my Colt, and flung the door open at the same time.

Tall, arthritic Fred Keogh had his right fist up high.

"You're quick," he drawled. "I ain't even knocked yet." He could see Skofer plain enough.

"Come on in, Fred," I said, holstering the forty-four. "I thought you were a prowler."

"Evenin', Mr. Haavik—or is it Pierpont?" Fred Keogh smiled.

"Just call me Skofer."

"Can I ask how come you're two people?"

"It's legal," I said. "We're just tryin' to be double damned sure the baron's packin' house scheme is real before we put any money into it."

"If I had two dimes to rub together, I'd likely do the same," he said with a nod.

"We'd just as soon nobody knew about it for a couple of days," Skofer said carefully.

"I don't talk, so long as it's legal," Keogh said gruffly.

"What can I do for you?" I asked, motioning him to a straight-backed chair against the wall.

"I'm some concerned about our marshal. He ain't come back yet, and the town's more than I care to handle on my own."

"Don't ask me to face that pack of loco cowboys!" I held up both hands to push the whole idea back where it came from.

"I kind of figured maybe we could get you the marshal's badge," Keogh said intently.

"Thanks, Fred," I said, "but I'm gettin' a little broad in the brisket and slow in the head."

"Not from what I hear about you and Rafe Egan." Keogh held on.

"I didn't have any choice," I said, "and I was lucky I was horseback."

"Quicker'n a greased black snake in August, they say." He smiled.

"I can't do it. We'll be movin' on in a few days."

"Thank you for your time, gents." Keogh stood up, creaked toward the door, and went on out.

I counted twenty and opened the door. The hallway was empty.

"What do you make of that?" I asked.

"Nothing." Skofer shrugged. "He's scared he can't handle the town, and rightly so."

"I tried marshaling," I said. "Didn't like it."

"Too much blood?" Skofer asked.

"Yes, that, but worse, it was blood from my own people. Cowboys are my kind of folks. Storekeepers, lawyers, and bankers are somethin' else."

"Don't get all fashed up about it."

"How long you think he was out there listenin'?" I muttered.

"Can't even guess."

"He might know he's on the list of suspects," I said, pacing back and forth.

"Time to get back. They'll be wondering what happened to me," Skofer said, and he went to the door. "You be careful, Sam."

"You're the one mixed up in a million-dollar swindle." I patted his bony shoulder. "Run at the first sign of trouble."

He slipped quietly out the door, and I paced the room some more. I'd lost all desire to sleep. It was a great idea while it lasted, I thought, pulling on my boots.

I figured if I was going to walk the floor all night I might as well take a walk over toward the river.

Down by the Long Branch and the New Elephant the cowboys were hooting and hollering. Some of them were doing stunts on their ponies, and once in a while somebody'd try to shoot out a star, but down at this end of town it was dark and quiet.

I crossed over the tracks into Nauchtown and saw the red-lighted cribs with cowboys staggering in and out, not quite sure where they were, or even why. The one thing on their minds, God love them, was they were going to stick to hell-raising until they whipped it to flinderjigs.

Polly's hitch rail was full, and the cranberry lamps over the door cast an eerie vermilion stain on the moonlit street as I walked on by.

I thought if I lived through the night, I'd have breakfast with Clarissa in the morning.

As I was fading off into the shadows a cowboy staggered out of Polly's, saw the movement, and yelled, "There's the sonsabitchin' coyote!"

He drew clumsily and fired in my general direction, the bullet moaning as it went off toward the cattle pens.

When does it stop? I wondered. Will it ever be peaceable and decent?

Bible says iron sharpeneth iron, and I'd been up against enough iron over the years to be honed fairly fine by now.

When is it going to let up, though? I wondered. Is it going to stay like this until you're stiff and cold? What the hell kind of a life is that?

Where's my loving housewife and little sprouts hanging around my neck?

They're lying up there, weathering away in the Valley of Many Mink, said the stars twinkling overhead. They're over and done with, the moon sang in wavering, ghostly tones.

"Like hell," I snarled to myself, mad that I could drift off into such a dreamland that drained a man's strength.

Somewhere there was a woman for me, a good one, and I wasn't so old I couldn't start some young ones, either. There was the valley of San Juan Bautista I'd seen that looked like the best cattle ground in all of California.

Sunny, clean, the Pajaro River cutting through. Owned by Doña Encarnacion Sanchez, a widow so beautiful she was the whole cake with the icing and goblets of wine around it.

Sam, you strange man, why aren't you with Doña Encarnacion playing fantan or Pedro in her drawing room in her big hacienda by the mission instead of prowling through Dodge City's dump?

I wondered about that, smiled at myself, and shook my head. I meant to get back to San Juan Bautista all right. It was just taking me a little longer to get started than I'd thought.

Doña Encarnacion had already had four husbands die on her, and she wasn't twenty years old yet. Suppose she took another husband? Likely he'd be a goner before I got back, and I could be the next candidate.

Thinking about it as I rambled through the shadows toward the river, it didn't sound too smart. Doña Encarnacion did indeed have the grandest ranch in California, but she also had a high death rate among her husbands.

Kind of like the male spider thinking he could have fun with the pretty little black widow.

Near the riverbank I found a clump of chokecherry bushes and hunkered down to watch. The yellow moonlight flooded the bare ground between me and the camp, rising and falling in waves.

The locusts buzzed like a thousand dancing rattlesnakes, their chorus meandering back and forth, rising and falling in intensity like the waves of the moon. Poorwills called, and little prairie owls hooted, trying to stir up a meal, and the town dogs barked in the distance while the coyotes howled their own paean out on the prairie, listening to and answering the moon.

The small campfires of the Indians glowed along the riverbank, and occasionally I'd hear a yell and a yelp as a small fight started and ended.

I wondered where they bought their alcohol. Where did the money come from? I doubted if many of the squaws could sell a poke to a nervous cowboy, but once the cowboy was blind drunk it was easy for him to poke anything with a hole in it, including a board fence. The alcohol probably came from the back doors of the saloons where leftover drinks were funneled into pint bottles.

Maybe they found enough trinkets they could trade for the rough stuff. Maybe they stole anything loose in their wanderings about town.

For sure it didn't take much to keep their brains as chopped up and pickled as sauerkraut.

The moonlight wavered hypnotically, like shining gold dust before my eyes. The humped-over figure was there, but I didn't count it in my head until it came across the far edge of the open area trudging toward the river camp, bent over, some kind of a box or bundle on its shoulder.

It could be a man or woman. It could be a white or an Indian. Only way to know was to get closer and meet it face to face.

I snaked around to my left toward the riverbank and, staying in the cover, made an arc to intercept the humped-over walker. Footing was tricky in the soft silt, but it made quiet going so that I ran without a sound to confront the ghostly walker. Not waiting,

I broke from my cover, charged across the moonlit open ground and, with my arms wide, drove the humpback to the ground.

A tin box landed so hard the lid fell off. I started a right fist to the jaw when I smelled smoky sour decay, a familiar blend to me now, and I jumped away in a panic.

"Mary, what the hell are you doin' out here?" I asked, brushing the front of my shirt in case some of her lice had jumped onto me.

"Heap scared," she groaned, sitting up.

"What have you got in that box?"

"Bread in box. Back of house," she said. "Fuckee two bits?"

8

IN THE SOUTHEAST NOW THE SEPTEMBER SUN LIFTED without summer's strength or fervor, each day more distant, more languid and inconsequential. A flat, dark cloud shaped like a giant scythe reached over from the horizon as if it might swoop down and gather up the whole prairie in its grasp and hook it back over the eastern horizon.

The rising sun and the purple-limned hook of cloud reminded me of something coming for me, and I wasn't ready yet.

Main Street hosted a flock of pigeons searching through the clumps of horse manure and a single hatless cowboy looking for a horse that wasn't there.

"Where'd he go?" he muttered with stunned eyes

as I passed by. "I told that danged broomtail to stay right there."

I walked over to Polly's Palace and knocked on the back door.

"Your breakfasts are better'n Delmonico's," I said to tall, limber-limbed Clarissa as she let me in.

She poured me a cup of coffee and said, "Quite a commotion over by the Injun camp last night."

"I was there," I said. "It didn't amount to much."

"I was afraid there'd been another knifing," she said over her shoulder as she ladled flapjack batter onto the griddle. "I was too busy running up and down the stairs and fetching cigars from uptown to go out and look."

"Better stay away from there. The gent with the knife might make a mistake."

"Mr. Benbow," she said, laughing, "when I see a blade I jump higher than a bullfrog and scat quicker'n a green racer."

"Just so you see him first."

She put a dish of stewed prunes in front of me and went back to stoke up the stove. "I did see something strange, though, when I shooed the last gent out the front door."

"A man with a box on his shoulder?" I smiled.

"No, it was an animal, a long one. I guess it was a big old longhorn got loose from the pens. Hard to tell in the dark."

"Pretty hard to jump a seven-foot corral, too," I murmured as she put a plate of flapjacks and fried ham next to the prunes.

"It looked big, though. Longest gentleman cow I ever seen, if that what it was."

"Clarissa," I said suddenly as a sharp knife edge of fear flashed through my mind, "you don't go outside at night anymore. Not even in the yard. Understand?"

"I hear you, Mr. Benbow"—she chuckled—"but I ain't worried about no bogey man. My head ain't blossoming for the grave yet."

"There's a plain-out maniac loose in this town, Clarissa," I said. "I've got to find him."

"If I could help, I would." She looked at me straight across, her dark eyes as honest as any woman's.

"You must hear stories about strange clientele," I said, watching her.

"Oh, that kind!" She poured out some of that thick, chocolaty laughter and nodded. "It ain't just men, either."

"Tell me," I said. "I need names."

"Well, there's that big man, they call him the baron. He likes a girl to squat down on his face and scratch his beard. That's passing strange to me. There's Doc Shreich. When he come over on Mondays to check the ladies he like to watch 'em play together. That dunghill gentleman, the ex-major that hangs around? He like a girl to pee in his ear. Then there's that old dude, Skofer Pierpont. He get drunk, he want all the girls in the bed with him. Still he a heap of stir and no biscuits. . . ." She paused to think of some more and added, "'Course, there's more, but they drummers or soldiers just passing through town. I guess I could mention the banker—what's his name?"

"Kennefik," I prompted her.

"They say he grins like a baked possum if you just pat his bare butt with a house slipper."

"Nobody's extra mean?" I asked, a little disappointed.

"Not among the locals just now," Clarissa said. "Polly won't put up with them kind."

"Thanks, Clarissa," I said, going out the back door and taking a deep breath of the fresh morning air.

Over in the area that Clarissa could see from the front door I looked for tracks. It was a scrubby patch of unused land; not much there except a broken china doll, a wrinkled, worn-out boot with the sole wired onto the top, and the marks in the dirt where I'd tackled Mary. The bread box was gone. There were other footprints pressed on top of hers and mine. For sure there were no hoof prints of a giant longhorn bull.

Maybe she'd seen something else in the dim moonlight, a wagonload of hay, maybe a polka-dotted pink elephant—*Quién sabe?*

Something about the morning disturbed me until I recalled it was too quiet. There were no cattle in the pens bawling out their discontent. It looked like the last of the Circle M cows were being loaded aboard a string of cattle cars. I went around to the tally master keeping track of the count and the herders with poles jabbing the cows into corridors that led to a long chute that angled up to fit the open cattle car door. It looked like the herd would be fully loaded and underway in a few minutes.

I went on around to the office and found Joe McCoy behind the counter going over a set of tally books.

Looking up at me, he said, "Just the man I'm looking for."

When somebody says something like that I always figure it's time to light a shuck and hightail it elsewhere, but there was no escaping his stern, deep-set eyes.

"At your service," I said.

"Something's wrong in the tally again. It looks to me like we're short two head from the Circle M herd."

"People make mistakes, even tallymen."

"It's true, but a couple of weeks ago the Turkey Track was short three head when they shipped out, and the Circle C was short one before then. It should average out, but it's always short on our end."

"You tally 'em when they come into the pens?" I asked.

"You know the system," he said.

"You separate them into different grades, from prime beeves to late calves?"

Again he nodded.

"Then you tally 'em one more time when they go up the chute into the car."

"That's it." McCoy shook his head and frowned. "The last count is running short too damn often. It won't break us, but it's not right."

"A few must die for one reason or other while they're in the pens."

"Once in a while there'll be a weak one or a goring," he said, "but generally it doesn't happen."

"You have guards patrolling at night?"

"Old man Faraday," McCoy said.

"Be pretty hard to steal 'em out of the pens."

"Unless it's those damned Injuns eatin' 'em inside out!" he muttered. "If you were still a brand inspector . . ."

"Mr. McCoy," I said carefully. "I sort of misstated my position the other day."

"Why?" He frowned. "There was only the baron and . . ." He stopped and stared at me. "The baron?"

"I'd go a little slow putting money into his syndicate," I said quietly. He was too experienced a man to ask anything more. "Please, not a word," I murmured, looking into his dark, unyielding eyes.

"You have my promise," he said heavily, and he tapped the tally book. "Can you look around for these?"

"I've got a notion." I nodded.

Outside a line of longhorns trudged along six abreast toward the big gates at the west end of the pens. They would be John Slaughter's herd of Double-Mill Irons coming in from the Big Pasture just as the last of the Circle Ms was put aboard the last car of the long train.

Walking through the empty pens, I made sure I knew the layout, which was simply a complex of corrals with wide gates. The keys to the smooth loading operation were the gates made of rough-sawn timbers and hung from posts with heavy blacksmithed hinges. By using those many gates the pen master could create space or an alley of any size he needed.

I looked for something extraordinary, but there wasn't much to see except water and feed troughs and a lot of cow manure. There were no dead animals stomped into the ground.

I worked on through the pens to the south side, which would be the hardest to watch at night. For no reason that I could think of, six gates were built into that side. They might be used to bring in cattle that had somehow gotten over the fence, or strays that hadn't come in with the main herd, but it looked to me like they were put there in case McCoy wanted to add on more pens, part of a long-term plan. For sure the pens were already overworked.

I looked at each gate and found the chains rusty, padlocks corroding, hinges dusty. None had been opened since the pens were first built.

The bottom rail on the fourth pen from the west showed a dark brown stain that could have been most anything, but it looked fresh, and it wasn't calf splatter.

I crawled through the railings and studied the ground, which was covered by a layer of cow manure packed down by the hard hooves of longhorns passing through. Near the railing I saw part of a boot print, then another.

I worked on the boot prints until I figured one of the pair had once been a walking boot with a low heel, and the other was simply a brogan, the type worn by farmers, with the soles almost worn through.

They were similar to those that had stepped over Mary's and my tracks the night before, and the same as the pair that had used the rowboat.

I felt a little sick to the stomach when I realized these cow thieves might just as well be killing any Indian squaws that happened to get in the way.

It wasn't any spotted elephant or giant longhorn bull that Clarissa had seen early in the morning. It had been two people with a calf carcass hanging from a pole on their shoulders.

The rest should be easy, and there was no hurry because the Double-Mill Irons would be too spooky to get near on their first night in the pens.

I went on around to the telegraph office at the depot and spoke to the pale, long-faced wireman. He checked through his undelivered telegrams and handed one over to me.

"Came in early this morning," he said, puffing on a blackened corncob pipe. "I couldn't make much sense of it."

I read the message, and I glanced at him, wondering if he was being paid by somebody or was just naturally nosy.

"Sometimes the old lady gets so drunk she can't spell cat," I said, and I took the yellow message page outside to read again.

CANDIDATE/WORTH MONEY YOU/LOVE MA.

It was simple enough. The baron was wanted. There was a reward.

It confirmed what I'd already guessed, but I was glad to know we were on the right track. I thought I'd better find Skofer and cut him out of the game.

I looked at the sun and realized Skofer would still be in bed. I heard the rising volume of bawling cattle showing fight at being removed from the lush open range and crowded in with too many other wild ones.

That meant the other herds would be coming closer, including the Cherry cows, which could be the Terrazas herd overbranded with the cherry and stem.

A long ride.

Get busy, Sam, I thought. Earn your wage. Pay out your life.

I took the steeldust out of the livery and rode slowly southwesterly, giving him plenty of time to loosen up the muscles that had been immobilized in the stall. He didn't want to hold back, but he enjoyed showing how well he minded about as much as he liked to run.

After two miles of walk and trot I put steeldusty into an easy gallop that ate up the grassy miles. We passed by the NS and the Frying Pan and the Rocking Chair without stopping, raising a hand once in a while to a distant outrider to let him know I was friendly but had business elsewhere. Then, pastured not far from a bend in the river, I saw another herd of varicolored linebacked longhorns.

Without being too obvious about it I managed to ride close enough to a few head and saw they wore the Cherry on the left hip, and the left ear was fully cropped.

I kept clear of the cattle after that, not wanting any of the hands to get contrary.

The camp was next to the river and was laid out like all the rest, with the chuck wagon its hub. A tarp had been strung between some cottonwoods to make shade for the punchers' bedrolls, and the cook, a short, fat black man, had his fire going in a fire ring.

The remuda grazed under the eye of the wrangler on upstream, and three horses were saddled and tied to the wagon tongue.

Around the fire hunkered four men with coffee mugs cupped in their hands. The oldest one was too raggedy-assed to be the owner, and I couldn't guess who was boss from the plain looks of the others as I rode close.

"Howdy!" I greeted them.

After a moment a very hard-looking man with a bent nose rasped, "Light down and have some coffee."

The boss was younger than thirty and wore a big, heavy Stetson that sagged with age. His face was mostly chiseled bone covered by tight-stretched sunburned skin. His eyes had that empty don't-give-a-damn look, flat and as unreadable as the black eyes of a pit viper. His mouth was a sardonic crack in a stone wall, thin, tough, cruel. His voice droned off-key, nasal, probably because of the broken nose. If I'd had my druthers, I'd'a said, "Thanks, but I'm in a hurry to get on a ways before dark."

Instead I said, "Much obliged," dismounted,

ground-tied the steeldust, and accepted a mug of black coffee from the cook.

"Good-lookin' horse," the boss commented in the nasal, raspy voice.

"He'll do," I replied.

There was a still time while they looked me over out of the corners of their eyes, and then the sharp-faced boss said, "Name's Cherry. Arnold Cherry. That's my brand." He didn't move or stick out his hand.

"Sam Benbow," I said. "It's an easy brand to read in poor light and won't hair over in winter."

Cherry nodded and sucked at his coffee noisily. "Business out this way?"

"Lookin' for a couple friends named Allison and Hardin."

"Not in my crew."

"They'd be comin' up from Hudspeth County."

"West of us. We're Jeff Davis County," Cherry said shortly, finishing up the confab, his thin lips clamped together like he'd locked an iron safe.

"Thanks for the coffee," I said. I handed the empty mug to the cook and mounted up.

"How many herds betwixt us and town?" the battered, tattered old cowpoke called out to me.

"I counted three," I said. "They're runnin' 'em through the pens pretty fast."

"By golly, I just can't hardly wait!" He grinned, showing his snaggy teeth.

"Wait for what?" I asked.

"Why, mister," he cackled, "I just can't hardly wait to jig old Polly around the ballroom again."

"Good luck." I smiled and rode off to the north between the remuda and the herd, then, once clear, turned the steeldust and put him on a straight line back toward Dodge.

From my experience, Arnold Cherry was an obvious mavericker set on making a fortune while his running iron was hot. I'd seen a dozen of them. Hard men, raised poor or lost the home place in the war, making up their minds that they'd break through the poverty no matter what. They'd brand any mavericks they could find and any other branded cattle, if they thought they had enough guns.

They had to be hard, though—harder than anybody else—to make a go of it.

It looked to me like Arnold Cherry was close to winning his gamble. The only way he could be proved a shady mavericker would be to shoot one of his cows, skin it, and look at the hide from the inside out. A different brand under his cherry would put a rope around his neck, but I wasn't authorized to kill his cattle, and neither was anyone else. It was like inviting yourself to get killed legal.

Stabling the steeldust, I thought of my list of candidates for the murder of the squaws and reckoned it was time to find Moon Gould. He was the only one on the list I hadn't talked to yet, and all the others were looking more innocent every day.

Major Hawes had said Gould was a gambler, halfbreed, thief, scum. Had few kinds words for Moon Gould. Like to see him dead and piss on his grave. Not highly regarded.

There were half a dozen gambling joints on both sides of the tracks.

Short, broad-shouldered, swarthy, pockmarked face, blue eyes, wears a red bandanna around his auburn hair.

I looked through Brennan's Gaming Room, which at that time of day was nearly empty. The rannies would be bucking the tiger later on after they'd had time for a few drinks of panther potion and drowned common sense. A few doors down a tent on a vacant lot held a chuck-a-luck table and a faro layout, but Gould wasn't among the dealers or shills.

It wasn't till I'd crossed over to Nauchtown and went into a long makeshift hall named Harry's Lucky Horseshoe that I found him. Gould was not playing the fixed wheels or the loaded dice or the jimmied monte box; he was at least that smart. I wondered, though, how a man who knew that every game and layout in the place had been rigged to cheat, how could he think the cards he was playing with weren't altered in the same way.

It was still early enough so that dealers were sometimes idle at the tables, but the poker table where Moon Gould sat was filled up with players. How many of them were professionals in cahoots was anybody's guess. It was their trade to mislead innocents, and they'd starve to death or die from a sudden bullet if they weren't good at it. I glanced around and spotted an average-sized man in a gray suit unobtrusively sitting on a high stool in the corner, gazing out over the room. That would be Harry making sure he didn't lose any money.

Gould wore buckskins, fringed, greasy, and a red rag around his head. He was slumped down in his chair, holding his cards high on his chest, his eyes moving around like blue darters, assaying the facial expression of each of his opponents.

"Raise you five," he said, and he pushed five cartwheels into the pot. It was the last of the money on the table in front of him.

"Call," the tinhorn across the table said.

"You've got to beat three jacks," Gould snapped, spreading his cards out on the table.

"Queens will," the gent said, laying his three ladies over the jacks.

"Shitfire," Gould growled, and he pushed back his chair and glared at the derbied man pulling in the pot. "How the hell can you draw two queens?"

"I didn't deal." The derbied man smiled. "Ask the man."

Gould started to add something to his protest, but—already breaching the table's code of etiquette—he was close to getting a small-caliber bullet between his blue eyes.

He clamped his wide mouth shut, got to his feet, and went to the bar.

I saw Harry's face twitch as the barrel-shaped bartender looked over at him, and when Gould ordered a drink of whiskey the bartender said, "I've got to see the color of your money."

"What the goddamn hell!" Gould screeched, glaring over at Harry, who was carefully looking the other way as if lost in thought.

"May I buy you a drink, my friend?" I asked,

moving in alongside the squat halfbreed, trying to sound like a dude just off the train.

He looked up at me, still mad and unsure of himself. It took a couple of seconds to decide I was such a nice man I'd be easy to handle. After all, I had the money, and he didn't.

"Thanks," he said. "I'm a little short just now."

I flipped a silver dollar onto the bar so that Harry wouldn't strain his eyes and said, "Tennessee, from a new bottle."

The barkeep looked at me grumpily, rummaged under the plank bar, and found a bottle of Micah McClanahan's best sour mash bourbon, poured our glasses full, took my dollar, and didn't give me back any change.

"Stuff's expensive," Gould said.

"It's just money." I smiled. "My father's a banker in Philadelphia."

"I admire the high class," he said, sipping the drink with his little finger stuck out like it had a busted knuckle.

"I'd like to talk with you, Mr. Moon," I said quietly.

He looked up at me suddenly, not with happy avarice, but with quick and unmistakable fear.

"Who gave you my name?"

"A man I met on the train. I'm interested in Indians."

"I ain't an Indian." He gulped down the drink. "I'm half white. My dad was a Methodist preacher."

"I guess that's close enough." I laid another cartwheel on the bar and nodded to the bartender for a refill.

"I don't like Indians," he said stubbornly. "I bet I've killed more goddamned Indians than anybody else in this place."

I nodded solemnly.

"In battle. Hand to hand. Ambush. I don't care, you name it, I'm certain death to the sonsabitches, and they stay the hell away from me."

"Women? Kids?" I drawled.

"Damn right. Lice make nits and nits make lice," he said sullenly. "An Injun is an Injun, and the only good one is a dead one."

"Is it very hard to kill an Indian?" I asked bashfully.

"You want to kill an Injun before they're all gone?" He grinned. "If you got the money, I'll set it up for you."

"I guess I'd like to go first class. How much would a chief cost me?" I asked softly.

"Chiefs are scarce around here," he whispered. "They ain't hardly any left. How about a good-sized buck? A real warrior?"

"How would we do it?"

"I tell him I've got a bottle of firewater. He comes along to some quiet place and drinks the bottle. When he falls over dead drunk you kill him. Simple."

"What'd that cost?"

"A hundred dollars."

"That's a little steep," I said. "How much would a squaw be?"

"Hell, I can get you a squaw for fifty. Tonight, if you're in a hurry."

"Could I use my six-shooter?" I asked, hoping I'd sound like one of Yale's finest bastards.

"I dunno . . ." He shook his head doubtfully. "You make a lot of noise close to town, might stir up trouble. Better use a knife."

"I haven't got a knife."

"You can borrow mine." He smiled, putting his hand on the bone handle of a scabbarded bowie.

"When?"

"It's real close"—he grinned—"just around the corner."

"Maybe we should talk outside," I said, looking around at the growing crowd.

"I know a man," he said quietly to me as we walked toward the door, "for another fifty dollars, he'll tan any part of her you want to keep for a souvenir."

"A trophy for the Skull and Bones." I nodded, a foolish smile on my ugly face.

— 9 —

OUTSIDE, MOON LOOKED UP AND DOWN THE STREET and moved away from the coal-oil lanterns lighting the Harry's Lucky Horseshoe sign.

"Where's the money?" he asked, his heavy shoulders sloping forward combatively.

"Have you ever done this before?" I asked.

"No more talk," he growled. "Now it's cash."

"But how do I know you'll carry out your end of the bargain?" I still tried to play dumb, but he was suspicious now, and impatient.

"I ain't sayin' no more," he growled. "There's somethin' about you smells like wolf bait."

"Me?" I tried to giggle.

"Mister, I'm goin' to find out what color your backbone is," he snarled, and a small thirty-six Colt slid into his hand from inside his buckskin jacket slick as fat blood.

If I hadn't been expecting the move, it would have worked well for him, but before he could bring the navy Colt to bear I had his wrist in both hands. One hard twist and the Colt fell to the ground.

Not waiting, I bulled him out of the light. He tried to squirm away, but I still had a bunch of his coat in my left hand, and I didn't mean to lose him. I bounced an overhand right off the back of the neck, and he pretended to slump and fall. I double-hooked him in the ribs, and he grunted like a pig, but he didn't give up. Those short, square-built ones tend to have something extra. He tried slipping out of his coat, but my knee slammed into his face and popped him back in the sleeves again. Up until then he'd just wanted to get away.

The bowie came out of nowhere and gleamed in the pale moonlight like a sliver of ice. He tried to come in low with it, but I jerked him sideways and brought across as hard a right as I had just below the red rag around his head. If he'd been an ox, it would've killed him. I decided his head was harder than my fist, and as he swung the knife again toward my midsection I sucked in my belly and jerked him off balance.

He was compact and quick, and I was running out of wind.

He tried an upthrust, and I took the chance of losing him by letting go of his coat and going for his wrist with both hands. He tried to twist away as I lifted his knife hand high so that he was touching the ground with his toes. Then I brought my right knee up and cracked his nuts.

He moaned, and the knife fell.

Still gripping his right wrist, I slowly eased him to the ground, where he grabbed his crotch and groaned like a bogged bull.

"Now, Mr. Moon," I wheezed, "we're goin' to have a little talk."

"Who are you? What do you want?" he choked out.

"I want to know how many squaws you put the knife to."

"Mister, I ain't touched any of them lousy Indians."

"You sold them to anybody that wanted a trophy," I said, already knowing it didn't make sense. All the derelicts had been expertly killed in the same way and by the same man.

"You asked the questions in at Harry's, I just give back the answers you wanted," Moon said with less pain and more anger.

"One of them was knifed two nights ago. Where were you?" I grabbed his coat front just in case he wanted to make a run for it again.

"Listen to me, big man," he said softly, "two nights ago I was tryin' to rob a train just west of Salina."

"That's where you got your gambling money?"

"There wasn't much. I was passin' the hat amongst the passengers and only had a few dollars and a couple of tin watches when some female buzzard came at me. Looked like a good honest church-goin' woman, but when I told her to empty out her purse she pulled a damn hatpin and went for my eyes.

"Once I backed up, everybody was onto me, and I just barely got off that train alive."

"Can you prove it?"

"Would I make up a story like that? Check the Salina *Journal.* It should be on the first page," he muttered bitterly. "Damn church-goin' women and their hatpins all to hell!"

I didn't think he was smart enough in his present condition to make up the yarn, and I had the sinking feeling that he was telling the truth.

"Who's killin' those women if it's not you?"

"How should I know? I just got into town. Hell, I had to walk damn near to Ellsworth before I could steal a horse."

"I ought to hand you over to the law," I said, knowing already I wasn't going to bother with him. He was such a failure as a liar, cheat, and holdup artist, I figured he wouldn't live much longer anyway.

"I'll give you somethin' free," he snarled. "There's a story floatin' around that your knife man is dressed all in black and has a hump back."

"Thanks for nothin'," I said. "Better you get out of town in short order before I change my mind about you."

"I haven't got a dime to travel on," he whined. "Could you loan me five dollars?"

"No," I said, walking back to the dimly lighted

street, disgusted with myself for being stupid, short of wind, and overweight.

Half a block down the narrow street I could hear music and singing echoing out of Polly's Palace and instantly thought of Skofer.

By now he'd be running short of the right answers. I should have pulled him out of the baron's reach before now, I thought. It had been too busy a day.

I rambled down the grubby lane past the cribs where the older sporters ended up leaning out the windows selling whatever they had left, like it was a secondhand store having a going-out-of-business sale.

The front door was locked, so I used the brass door knocker. Clarissa, wearing a shiny black dress and a little white lace apron, opened the door and said formally, "Good evenin', Mr. Benbow. There is a one dollar admission fee."

I gave her the dollar and asked, "Why?"

"Keeps out the riffraff." She giggled and covered her mouth with her hand.

She opened the door to the main room and whispered with a smile, "This is what they call the ballroom."

I heard a familiar voice singing and then saw Skofer banging a spinet piano with a young lady on either side of him, singing:

"The bosun's mate was very sedate,
Yet fond of amusement, too—
He played hopscotch with the starboard watch
While the captain tickled the crew.

And the gunner we had was apparently mad,
For he sat on the after rail-ail-ail . . .
And fired salutes from the captain's boots
In the teeth of the booming gale!"

When Skofer reached the chorus he stood and banged on the piano with his right hand and waved his other hand at the audience, exhorting them to join in.

I looked over the audience and saw the bald-domed baron bulging out all over, stolid and unresponsive as an anvil. Beside him at the table were Hastings and Kennefik, who looked like a toad with sideburns. Slightly to the rear of them sat the gunsel they called Snake. Facing them across the table and with their bare backs to me were three females. At a table in the corner ex–Major Fred Hawes and a red-haired trooper of equal temper gloomily watched the proceedings, as if it was the first time they'd ever been in a high-class whorehouse and had to pretend it was scandalous. At another table sat two drummers more interested in talking to the ladies than hearing a wobbly gray-haired, eccentric financier caterwaul.

If looks could kill, the baron's glare would have vaporized Skofer.

Was he mad because Skofer was playing the fool, or had he somehow figured out his game?

I couldn't very well drag Skofer out by his shirt collar, which was now unbuttoned, the string tie loose and drooping.

Still, I wanted to warn him to get clear of the baron's crew as quick as he could.

I moved in unobtrusively to a table in the other corner.

"Some good whiskey," I said to Clarissa, sitting down.

As soon as Clarissa left, her place was filled by a tall, big-boned, red-haired woman wearing a long red ruffled dress with most of the bosom cut out. I hadn't seen a sight like that since I was weaned.

She sat down next to me and said with a big horse-tooth smile, "Evenin', cowboy. I'm Polly in the flesh, and don't ask me if I want a cracker."

"The girl is bringin' me a drink, Polly," I said, trying to see her true features in the dim candlelight. Her face carried such a thick coat of powder she might as well have been a statue made of pink sandstone. Her eyes were clear and sharp, and she had a long hooked nose, which maybe was responsible for the *nom d'amour* of Polly.

I thought if I hung around with her, I'd put a marker in my wallet. Chances are the marker would be there the next morning, but still you'd want to be sure about her.

It was just a thought. I wasn't going to hang around. If I wanted someone in Polly's Palace, I'd pick Clarissa, just because of her throaty, thick chocolate-drizzled chuckle.

"I wasn't talkin' about your drink," Polly said mildly, eyeing me with a little sense of humor showing in the corners of her red-smeared lips.

"I'm comfortable with you, Polly," I said

as Clarissa put the glass of bourbon in front of me.

"I like a gallant man." She laughed huskily and punched me on the shoulder. "Listen to that old coot sing!"

"He's a madcap all right."

> "I'm Captain Jinks of the Horse Marines
> I feed my horse on oats and beans . . .
> And when I take him out and put him to the cart,
> He spreads his legs and lets go a big . . . nei-ei-eigh!"

It looked to me like Skofer was just getting warmed up instead of playing out, what with his gusto and the ladies' hands swarming all over him, encouraging him one way or another.

Outside a killer could move through the crooked streets and alleys and do his dirty work, but you'd never know it from the ballroom.

"Don't he ever stop?" I asked Polly.

"We don't want him to stop." She grinned. "If he wasn't a millionaire, I'd hire him permanent."

"Millionaire? Him?" I shook my head.

"Take my word for it, cowboy. He's just havin' fun now."

"Shucks, I've never even seen a millionaire before, let alone an old goat capering around like a fat pony in a field of oats."

Ex–Major Hawes paid his bill and, with the

redheaded trooper, walked out of the room as if they were leaving the scene of Sodom, Gomorrah, Shadrach, Meshach, and Abednego.

The music changed, and I noticed Skofer fingering the piano keys tentatively on a new tune until he had it sorted out in his head, then he started that crazy "Stodola Pumpa."

"Three years to wait is much too long for us,
My love and I, we now could married be,
Ya, she and I we now would have a son,
Strong and handsome, handsome just like . . . *me!*"

Skofer jumped up on the piano bench and, facing us, waved his arms and shouted "Hey!" and in rapid time commenced the refrain,

"Stodola, stodola, stodola pumpa,
Stodola, stodola, stodola pumpa
Stodola pumpa, pum-pum-pum!"

He didn't really finish the last "pum" because a scream like a goat being torn to pieces by dogs rose and fell from outside.

I was on my feet when Polly grabbed my arm and said, "Take it easy, cowboy, it's just them damned Indians over by the river."

I dropped a cartwheel on the table and said, "I've heard that kind of yell before."

"What the blazes?" the baron barked.

I looked over and noticed he was sitting alone;

apparently Hastings and Kennefik had gone upstairs to play with the girls.

I ran like an aging antelope out into the street and off toward the river camp.

No one followed me.

Give Skofer credit, I thought—he had already started up another tune as I charged across the empty field toward the river.

I saw him in the faint moonlight going through the brush, a dark humped figure hurrying toward the railroad tracks.

"Hold it!" I yelled, and I went after him.

He was quick or I was slow. He was real or he was a phantom. He wasn't where I thought he should be, and it was useless to run around in the dark looking.

I ran back toward the camp where someone had thrown some scrap pine kindling on a fire for light. Someone had wanted to see, seen it, and gone off to be sick.

Off to the side Mary lay grotesquely on her back. Her ragged robe had been ripped open down the front. Her open eyes bulged with fear but were already dusty. Her toothless mouth was open in a rictus of horror. A T cut had been made in her lower abdomen in two strokes.

I turned her head to see the nape of her neck.

The three slits where fresh blood oozed showed so innocently, you'd have thought they were no more than scratches from a rosebush if you didn't know.

The killer had missed the first stab to the medulla, hitting bone instead, giving Mary enough time to scream out her terror. He hurried the second try and missed that one, probably holding her by her matted, crawling hair. The third stab with his stiletto slipped over the vertebra and cut into the heart of the brain. He'd made his abdominal cuts, but before he could go any further he'd heard me coming. Cheated of his real pleasure, no doubt he'd be back for more playthings as soon as he thought it was safe.

Could I see him again in my mind's eye? I tried, but nothing showed except a black shape against black shadow.

It wasn't the baron. I knew where he'd been when that death scream ripped loose, but I couldn't be sure about the rest.

The fat pine flared and burned down to a dim glow, and I walked back across the field to Nauch Row with names and faces swarming through my mind.

My first thought was that I'd left Moon Gould loose because of a yarn he could have cooked up freehand, and I was kicking my mental butt for that when I reached the open door of Harry's Lucky Horseshoe gambling emporium.

Before I reached the door a shot thumped and gusted out. I backed off to the side.

Gunplay inside a small room full of nervous people is nothing to stick around for. Patience has its rewards, one of them being survival.

I waited as the scrubby jaspers crowded outside, knowing the game as well as I did.

"What's goin' on?" I asked a seedy gambler in a rusty black frock coat.

"Holdup," he said nervously, watching the open door.

"That's crazy," I said. "Nobody's dumb enough to hold up a dive like this."

"You'd bet ten to one against, but you'd lose," he said.

The hall inside quieted down some, and a group of the curious waited with me until Harry, with what looked like the same cigar in his mouth, and a big overdressed gambler came out dragging the holdup man by the wrists.

They didn't stop until Moon Gould lay over on the shadowed vacant lot next door.

Moon had a small blue bullet hole just below his left eye.

Coming back, Harry slipped his thirty-six-caliber Colt back into the shoulder holster and grinned at the spectators.

"Come on, boys, the luck's changed now that we got rid of that jinx." No one moved. Harry puffed a little fire into his damp cigar, then tried again. "Come on, boys, everybody's a winner at Harry's! This one is on the house!"

That woke them up. The image of a dead Moon Gould was quickly replaced by a glass of free popskull, and they followed Harry inside just like sheep following a Judas goat into the slaughterhouse.

"Come along, friend," the tinhorn said, noticing me holding back.

"No, thanks."

"Friend of yours?"

"No more'n the rest of the losers in this world," I said, and I moved off into the darkness toward Polly's place.

There was no sound of gaiety echoing down the street from Polly's, but the red lamp was still burning over the front door.

Chances were they were all bedded down and going through the frolics by now. I wondered if it was going to cost me another dollar to go in again.

I wondered about that black, almost formless shape I'd seen hurrying through the darkness. Was there a hump on his back? Did he have a shiny tin box on his shoulder?

How many squaws were there left over in river camp that'd serve for bait? As I recalled, Mary was the last of the youngish females. Of course, there'd be others drifting in. Another week, there might be three or four new ones. Fuckee two bits. Goddammit to hell.

There was still a dim light from inside, but the door was locked. I rapped with the brass knocker until Clarissa opened it up. She looked at me and shook her head.

"We closed, Mr. Benbow."

"What happened to the party?"

"They ran out of songs," she said, looking down at the floor.

I saw Polly standing in the hall back in the shadows, listening.

"Polly, I don't believe it," I said. "I want to see that old man."

"That old man gone," Clarissa said apologetically, perhaps even sadly.

"Then I want to find him." I had my foot in the door, and there was no one in that house with a bigger foot.

"Go away, Mr. Benbow," Clarissa pleaded softly.

"Polly," I said loudly, "I'm goin' to burn your shack down if I don't get any answers."

"You ain't goin' to burn nothin' down, cowboy," she growled, coming forward, shoving Clarissa aside, and at the same time leveling a rabbit-eared, sawed-off twelve-gauge two-bore at my middle. "You just git, mister, before I make cat meat out of you."

You can do it quick or you can talk 'em into getting careless, but it's not a good thing to have such a greener pointed at your middle, even if it isn't cocked. You've got to do something. I dropped to my knees, grabbed her big ankles, and, coming back up, threw her ass over teakettle out into the street.

The shotgun boomed once as she sailed.

"Holy jumping Jesus!" Clarissa yelled, and she started to run down the hall. I went for her fast, and I wasn't much nicer to her than I was with Madame Polly.

I caught one long, skinny arm, but that was enough. Setting my feet, I jerked hard and let her slam herself against the wall. Then I hit her on the ear when she tried to bite my hand.

"It doesn't need to be this way," I said. "Just tell me where they took him."

She looked at me with the whites of her eyes

showing and shook her head. "They'll kill me," she choked out.

I hit her again in the same place, and she muttered, "The office. That what they said. The office."

"Thanks, Clarissa. I'll be by for breakfast in the mornin'," I said gently, and I let her lean against the wall by herself.

I'm not one to go around hitting women for just anything, but I figure it don't hurt 'em much more'n it hurts a man, and usually it's a good experience. Makes 'em feel like they know where they belong and what they're supposed to be doing. They don't have to worry about whether somebody likes 'em or doesn't like 'em, should they be doing this or doing that, and getting all confused about life. Once they're stabilized with a knock or two on the side of the head they're always a lot happier. I've seen women just sing their hearts out for joy after the old man rapped 'em a couple of times to show he cared.

I met Polly at the doorway. She showed fight, and I was set to stabilize her, too, when she figured she'd had enough even before she'd had it.

She backed off and made a showy curtsy as I walked off the porch and turned toward the tracks.

It was a long hike for a buckaroo who's not accustomed to walking, and once I was on Front Street the going was slow because of the wild-eyed cowboys still crowding down the boardwalk arm in arm.

I was trying to get around a knot of peelers holding each other up when a big bearded buckaroo with leaden eyes grabbed me around the waist and said, "Sweetie, let's dance—"

I gave him both elbows to the ribs, and he stared at me anxiously and said, "Pardon me, ma'am, I didn't know your husband was with you."

Turning off the boardwalk, I passed between tethered ponies to the middle of the street, where there was less traffic.

The office of the Great Western Meat Products Company was across from the bank, tucked in between a saloon and the mercantile, and I legged it that way, cussing myself for not getting Skofer out of danger sooner.

My patience was some frayed and my temper on full cock. It's not a civilized way to be and is always downheartening to me later on when I think of how I could have done better. I was thinking along those lines, trying to calm down and be reasonable, when I came to the front door of the Great Western.

Slowly and quietly I tried the knob, but it didn't turn. I could kick the door open, or I could just break a pane of glass alongside it, reach in, and unlock it.

There must be other ways, I tried to tell myself, but then I heard a mad squall from far back in the building.

I rapped on the pane of glass with my gun barrel and reached around for the jigger to unset the lock, then I moved very quietly inside.

The front room was pitch black, and I drifted over

to the opposite corner first thing in case somebody in the back room had heard the glass break.

The door opened, revealing tall, lanky Snake with his forty-four in his hand, looking toward the open front door. His eyes weren't adjusted to the dark yet.

"Somebody there?" he asked, moving the Colt slowly back and forth.

I shot him twice without thinking. Man with a gun in his hand looking for you, you don't want him to find anything.

I heard footsteps and the back door slam as I warily approached.

"It's clear," Skofer groaned, and I stepped into the back room, where he lay sprawled in a corner.

I went over to the old coot with the mashed-in face.

"What took you so long?" He tried a grin but quit before it hurt.

"Figured you wanted to handle 'em by yourself."

He closed his eyes, and I saw how pale he was where his face wasn't bruised or cut.

"You broke up any?" I asked. His pulse stuttered along raggedly under my fingers.

"Hip poorly."

"What'd they want?"

"Mainly just who and what . . ." He tried to shake his head. "Somehow they figured me for a ringer."

"Who all?"

"Baron. Hastings. Snake," he whispered.

I picked him up and said, "I'm goin' to pack you over to the doc, then we can talk business."

His head slumped on my shoulder. I don't think he heard me.

This time I used the alley behind Main Street and carried the scrawny old goat up to the other end of town—all of three blocks—to Doc Shreich's place.

I kicked on the door until I heard someone moving inside.

In a moment the door opened, and the doc, in his long nightshirt and a mangy robe, holding a lamp high, looked at me, then at Skofer's pale, bloody face.

"Come in. What happened?" He clucked his tongue anxiously and backed off so I could carry Skofer into the examining room and put him on the same cot that I'd laid on a few days before.

"Some hombres been tryin' to wear him out," I said.

"Unconscious," the doc said first off. "He's in shock." Quickly he covered Skofer with two woolen blankets, drawing them up under his chin. "Anything broken, do you know?" he asked.

"He said his hip hurt."

Doc moved to the foot of the cot and turned each of Skofer's boots left, then right.

"Maybe a deep bruise," he said, shaking his head. "I don't think there's a fracture."

As he talked I noticed his tousled hair, his lined face, and his moth-eaten bathrobe and thought even doctors are mortal human beings sometimes.

"I can give him an injection?" He put it as a question, looking at me for a yes or no.

"Let's wait. He's had plenty of knocks in the head

before. I wouldn't think a couple more would hurt him serious."

He cleaned Skofer's face with a wet white cloth and nodded with satisfaction.

"No need for sutures," he said. "Some little scars maybe, but what's a few more to a man of that age?"

10

WITH THE ACRID ODOR OF ETHER, ALCOHOL, AND ACID burning the inside of my nose, I woke up on Doc's spare cot, and after I scrubbed my stubbly face in cold water I took a look at the still-sleeping Skofer, then glanced over at Doc Shreich at his desk, sorting through slips of notepaper and making notations in a leather-bound journal.

So concentrated and oblivious was he in his work, he didn't notice that I was up or say good morning.

Not wanting to disturb him, I moved quietly around the room, looking over the strange equipment. A long table covered with beakers and bottles stood to the side where two overhead lamps were still lighted. Against the wall was a hodgepodge of open shelves holding books, crystal bottles with glass stoppers, large covered jars labeled sulfuric and muriatic acid, alcohol, and other chemical names unfamiliar to me.

On the second shelf was a hand-cranked centrifuge, a large syringe, and some kind of a distiller, all made of glass.

A microscope was set up on the long table, and I squinted down through the lenses and saw some gray rings with black dots inside them.

"What do you call these things?" I asked.

Doc Shreich sighed tiredly, looking over the top of his spectacles at me, and said, "Those are blood cells. It's an old slide, so they're dead."

"If they were fresh, they'd be movin' around some?"

"A little," he said, nodding, and he went back to his book work.

Toward the center of the first shelf what looked like a copper-bound five-gallon keg lay on its side. It was unusual because it had hinges and a pair of handles that came together.

"What do you use this for, Doc?" I asked, undoing the simple hasp and opening the upper half. The bottom half was filled with what looked like ordinary water.

He looked up, a trace of irritation on his pale, lumpy features. "That's an instrument bath," he said. "That's salt water. After I've done an operation I put all the instruments in there. Microbes can't live on metal that's in a saline solution."

"Don't the steel rust?"

"Yes. The instruments have to be washed in clean,

hot water und dried after an hour's soak. That's why the bath is empty."

I let the lid down. "I hope I'm not botherin' you, Doc."

"Not at all," he said, going back to the slips of paper and the ledger.

Toward the end of the shelf stood an open wooden box with special shapes cut out to hold various small surgical instruments. The biggest one was a long, oversized corkscrew; the edges of the screw were honed sharp.

"This gadget?" I asked.

Politely holding his annoyance, he looked over and said quietly, "We use that surgical volute on syphilitic males. The long screw is wound up into the genito-urinary canal inside the penis, then quickly jerked out, tearing away scar tissue and chancrous material."

"That must smart some," I said, putting the long corkscrew carefully back in its case.

"Yes"—he nodded—"it is quite rigorous, und a powerful lesson to men who patronize loose women."

"Do you check the sporters in town regularly?"

"Every Monday," he said with a nod, "but that check is only applicable for the moment. An hour later a prostitute could be infected, und I wouldn't find it until the following Monday. Abstinence is the only way for unmarried men, I'm afraid." He smiled and bent his bald head over the ledger, then looked up again and added as an afterthought, "Of course, for women the infections are worse, because they usually can no longer bear children."

"I've known some women that would count that as a blessing," I said.

He put down his pen, took off his spectacles, rubbed his eyes, and stood up.

"Mr. Benbow, barren women are the bane of the world. Every childless woman is a troublemaker." He wasn't smiling. "I believe there would be no more imperial conquests or wars if every woman on this earth had her hands full taking care of her children. I've spent a good deal of time researching this historical problem, und there's no doubt about the conclusions."

"Pretty hard to change things like that," I said, not wanting to argue with him.

"It is the duty of science to change things for the better, und this area needs to be solved even if it takes the best minds in the world to do it. If we could lock Louis Pasteur, William Harvey, and a Joseph Lister in a laboratory und tell them they couldn't come out until they had the cure for sterile females, the problem would be solved within a year."

"Some folks might say they don't want anybody tinkerin' with God's work." I smiled.

"That's what makes the difference between a real scientist und a quack," he said somberly.

"I just never thought it was that serious."

"I'm sorry." He smiled. "I get carried away by the subject. But think about all the wars and troubles caused by infertile queens und courtesans that would have been avoided if they'd each had a dozen children. From Helen of Troy and Cleopatra to Napoleon's Josephine, the list is endless. . . ."

"You better get busy, Doc. Maybe you can be famous."

"I'd like to solve it, of course." He shook his head a little sadly and shrugged. "I'm trained to be a general practitioner, but if I had a laboratory back in Germany, I might make a stab at it."

He chuckled and went over to take Skofer's pulse.

Turning back to me, he said quietly, "Pulse is normal. His problem is exhaustion. A man his age shouldn't be out cavorting day and night."

"Somebody talking about me?" Skofer groaned, keeping his eyes closed.

"You get out of that bed, old man, before I take a pussy whip to you," I said gruffly.

"I already been pussy-whipped," he murmured. "I don't think I need any more."

Doc Shreich went to the foot of the cot and turned Skofer's left foot slowly one way and then the other. "Can you do that?" he asked.

"I guess," Skofer said, and he rotated the foot.

"Try the right one," Doc said.

The foot went over to the left, and, groaning, Skofer slowly turned it over to the right.

"Excellent." Doc smiled. "I was afraid you'd fractured the hip."

"It feels worse'n that," Skofer said.

"The sciatic nerve may be damaged. It can be quite painful."

"You need me for anything?" Skofer looked at me

like he'd climb out of his death bed and go to work if I said yes.

"No legwork," I said, "but I'd like to talk."

"Shoot." He lay back and closed his eyes as Doc returned to his desk and file boxes.

"Austin wired me that the baron is wanted."

"I know that now." Skofer tried to make a grin and failed. "Another thing interesting about him is that he speaks Spanish. Another is that he carries a pair of little two-shooters in his vest pockets."

"That all?"

"No, he also speaks the language of bankers and high finance people fluently. He could sure fool me with all his five-words-to-the-pound gargle. Another thing is that he doesn't drink. He buys, all right, but he manages to slop it away somewhere. Also, with women he claims he's the biggest stud horse on the prairie, but there's a rumor—"

"I heard it," I said. "Did he make the connection between you and me?"

"I don't think so. Once he started sniffing around, I let him think I was just looking for some easy money and figured he was my mark."

"Is there anything level about his meat-packin' plant?"

"He's got a few plans drawn up that make a pretty picture, but most of those rolled-up papers are blank, just window dressing."

"His cattle will come into the pens today. They'll start shipping tomorrow, likely," I said. "He's got to rope in his easy marks before that herd has gone east."

"Why would he be in such a hurry?" Skofer asked.

"There's inspectors in the slaughterhouse in Chicago."

"So?"

"They look at both sides of the hide."

"And if they see an overbrand they report it to the commander." Skofer nodded.

"By then the baron will be long gone."

"I guess we could just knock him in the head and haul him in."

"I doubt if Fred Keogh would stand for it." I shook my head.

"We could sneak in and cut a patch of hide off the butt of one of his cows—"

"There's guards, and besides, them *cimarrones* would tear you to pieces first."

I looked over my shoulder to see if Doc was listening, but he was engrossed in his ledger and files, concentrating like he was in another world.

"Maybe Hastings is a weak link," I said.

"My feeling was that him and the baron had teamed up years ago, and each trusted the other all the way." Skofer shook his head.

"Then it's a standoff."

"You any closer on what happened to the squaws?" he asked, and I told him about Moon Gould being the reason I was late catching up with him.

I didn't tell him about Clarissa and Polly. He's more sensitive to female frailties than I am.

There was a knock at the front door. Doc shook his head with exasperation and called out, "Come in."

I heard the street door open and close, then Fred Keogh ambled on arthritic knees through the anteroom on into our room.

"Looks crowded." Keogh smiled, all the spider-web lines on his face tightening upward.

"You're up early, Fred," the doc said. "If you've got a private problem, we can look at it in the other room."

"No, it's nothing, Doc," Keogh said quietly. "I just heard about Mr. Haavik falling into a barrelful of bobcats and thought I ought to take a look."

"Nothing wrong with me that a couple dancing girls won't cure!" Skofer protested.

"And you, Mr. Benbow, it seems you've been busy reducing our population." He looked over at me with his unreadable poker-chip eyes.

"It seems I've run into some folks that don't care for my manners," I said.

"I need two dollars from you for the gravedigger," he said.

I put a couple cartwheels in his hand and said, "That's pretty cheap."

"You get a discount when they all go in one grave," he said laconically. "Reckon I should have the grave-digger leave it open in case you're going to add on?"

"What about the squaw, Mary?" I asked.

"They don't permit squaws in our graveyard," he said. "Them people over at the river will scratch out a hole for her, likely."

"Likely." I nodded.

"I'll be glad when all them squaws are gone," he

said. "It'd suit me to hang 'em all and clean up the town."

"Hanging is a terrible way to execute a person," Doc murmured. "It should be forbidden by law."

"You got a better way, Doc?" Keogh made that wrinkled smile again.

"Definitely. If we're going to have public executions, I would insist on using a double-barreled ten-gauge shotgun loaded with double-ought buckshot fired point-blank at the head. In an instant the entire skull und every particle of brain matter would vaporize, and the victim would feel nothing."

"Not too many folks'd want to attend that sort of an exhibition," I said.

"Then I'd make it compulsory. All adults would have to view the dissolution of the man's upper extremities."

"You ain't serious," Keogh said.

"I'm deadly serious," Doc said strongly, his eyes gleaming behind the specs. "I believe in the betterment of mankind, and I think there are better ways to achieve that goal than hanging people by the neck."

"I got to respect your high-minded ideas, but I just don't think I'll miss any drinks waitin' for 'em to happen," Keogh said, heading for the door.

"I kinda like that idea of the shotgun, Doc," I said after he left. "It'd sure dampen the joyful executioners."

"There's more to it than that, of course," he said with a nod. "It's the basic concept of punitive law in this country und others that has to be rethought und changed."

"Changed how?" Skofer asked, lying back.

"It's simple," Doc said. "Common criminals, like common whores, are known to be deficient mentally either through heredity or some emotional shock. In a word, they are extra dumb. As it's set up now, they cannot compete or survive except by breaking laws made by smarter people."

"I never thought about it that way," Skofer said, "but there's some truth in it."

"The law penalizes und punishes the weakest of our people und rewards the privileged such as myself," Doc Shreich said strongly.

"How you goin' to fix it?" I asked.

"Very simple. Genuine public education. We've got to build more schools und fewer prisons."

"Tell that to the privileged politicians," Skofer said.

"Someday it has to come," Doc said.

While they talked I was thinking about some bacon and eggs and cinnamon rolls along with about a quart of coffee.

"I'm goin' to bring you some breakfast, Skofe," I said.

"Where you goin'?" he asked.

"Polly's."

"Figures." He yawned and closed his eyes.

"You want somethin', Doc?" I asked as I passed by his desk.

"No, thanks," he said, not looking up from the

paperwork spread out over his desk. "Coffee will give you dyspepsia."

Outside it was a toss-up whether it was easier to go over to the livery for the steeldust or walk over to Polly's. Either way was too slow for my appetite, which directed me to go down the street a few doors to Delmonico's.

I sat at the counter and asked for the works, but it wasn't the same as Clarissa's magic. They used the grounds twice to make the coffee. The flapjacks were sinkers, the eggs were fried hard, the bacon fat and chewy, and there weren't any cinnamon rolls. They didn't offer stewed prunes, either, which made us even.

I asked the waitress to send a hot plate over to the doc's office and paid the bill without enthusiasm.

Outside I sat on a bench in the weak sun, picking my teeth and watching the passing parade while my stomach juices did their best to reduce the grease-bucket breakfast into nutritional soup.

This early the street was mostly occupied with serious business. Wagons and carts hauled materials back and forth. Immigrants with their moon faces thunderstruck plodded up from the depot, carrying their bundles and bags. Tradesmen were unlocking the doors, and clerks were sweeping the boardwalk, sometimes throwing a bucket of water at a puddle of half-dried blood. All in all, a healthy, wholesome time of the day for Dodge City.

From the distance came the sorry wail of an eastbound freight train, and closer by, the roosters made their morning exultations and declarations with such fervor they had to believe they were keeping their world from falling off a cliff.

What the hell was I going to do with the baron? I figured I sure couldn't let him run off scot-free, but I didn't want to spook him either.

Thinking along those lines, I left my liar's bench and strolled over across the tracks to the broker's tally office. They were getting ready to load the baron's herd, but it would be a few hours yet.

Inside, Joe McCoy said good morning, looked at me hopefully, and asked, "You find out where those odd critters went?"

"I'm close," I said. "Would you be satisfied just to see it stopped, or do you want to hang somebody?"

He looked at me sternly and said, "Fix it."

"Yes, sir, I think I can do that," I said, then I added, "I'd like a favor."

"I guess I owe you a favor, Benbow," he said, frowning.

"No, you don't"—I smiled at him—"but it's partly a favor to yourself, too."

"I'll listen, at least," he said.

"Hold off payin' the baron until the last possible moment."

"You know the rules," he said. "When the last cow steps into the cattle car I give the seller my bank draft."

"Can't you say you're a little short, you'll have it the next day, somethin' like that?" I tried.

"No." He shook his head. "There should be cattle cars arriving this afternoon."

I looked over the pens full of Frying Pan cattle and

saw that they'd adapted to the crowding and had settled down some. Nothing for it but to do it the hard way.

I found the tall, pale telegrapher loading up his corncob with some Derby shag and said I'd like to send a wire. He shoved over a yellow piece of paper and an indelible pencil stub.

Took me a while to figure out how to get around his big nose and foxy eyes, and when he read it he said, "It don't make sense, even backwards. "NO CARAVANS TO SUNSET SEND. OMAR KHAYYAM."

I paid the sour-faced wireman and wondered how much the baron paid him to peek at my messages.

I wondered, too, if the commander had enough powerful friends to stop the cattle cars from coming out west to Dodge.

Feeling some better, I strolled back over to Main Street and considered the matter of whether a drink of Tennessee whiskey would make my stomach worse or cut the grease. A stabbing pain hit me in the belly as one of the sinkers with a sharp edge collided with a mummified egg and made up my mind for me.

Going through the door, I saw Maric trudging down the boardwalk as if lost in serious thought.

I stepped back and stood in his way so that he'd have to wake up and see me. After he said hello I said, "You looked like your mind was way off in western Montana."

"Likely was," he said slowly, his eyes steady but neither friendly or hostile.

"Come in and have a drink with me, clear out all the cobwebs."

"I don't mind," he said somberly.

Once we'd bellied up to the bar and been served I said, "No offense, but you seem kind of down at the mouth. Anything I can help you with?"

"I told you my yarn the other day," he said, drinking his beer thirstily. "Every day that goes by brings winter closer."

"Still want to open up your mine?"

"Sure do."

"You got a partner to help with the work?" I asked, tasting the Tennessee. At least it was better than breakfast. I was sorry now that I'd sent a plate over to Skofer. If he had any sense, he'd hide it under the bed.

"Partner?" Maric's eyes shifted. "I'm pretty much a loner. Man travels faster that way."

"Mighty lonely up on a mountainside in the winter."

"You got somethin' in your craw, Benbow?" His eyes firmed up, and his voice turned scratchy.

"Not me." I held up both hands and smiled. "I'm just commenting on the human condition, deplorable as it is."

"You took a squaw," he said, remembering.

"I didn't think of it that way."

"But you know how it is." He looked at me again, his expression altered to a sort of hopeless hope that I would understand what he was going through.

"Steady on," I said softly. "I know. Yes, I know."

"I'm poor ragged-ass broke," he said, dropping his eyes, "and I'm in the wrong place to make my livin'."

I nodded, saying nothing.

Sweat beaded his dark forehead, and his hands were moving around like twittering birds.

"You want me to guess?"

"No, Benbow," he said, straightening up and getting his shoulders back, "this goddamn civilization's damn near got me down, but I ain't whipped yet. I don't give a damn what you think. Fact is, my squaw followed after me clear to Missouri, and I been in quicksand ever since."

"But she's yours. You're her man. That right?"

"That's right, and nobody will come between us. She's stuck by me." He paused and swallowed and looked at the floor. "You must know how I feel."

"I do. I'd give my chance in heaven to hike the hills and valleys of the green parkland with my lady beside me," I said, dead serious.

"Goddammit, Benbow, how can it be so damned bad now after it was so damned good?"

"About all we can do is keep tryin'," I said. "Better to think about your silver mine."

"Mister," he said strongly, "I'm not askin' anything now from you. I'm just sayin' I've got to get my woman away from here and back to the mountains before we both drown in a bottle like them others."

"A man told me once that the hardest thing to figure out was what was the problem. Once you get that straight, then it's easy to figure out the solution."

"What a bunch of horseshit," he gritted, and he walked out the door.

I thought about it for a while and decided he was right. Poor folks may have poor ways, but they don't have any problems figuring out what their problem is. It's the solution that's always just over the next range of mountains.

— 11 —

OUT ON THE STREET I RECOGNIZED THE BARON'S hardcases scattered among the cowboys gathering for their night's blowout, but I saw no hell-for-leather grins of anticipation on their faces, which meant that they hadn't been paid off yet.

Coming to the depot, I went around to the telegraph office, and as I came in the door the voices stopped in midsentence.

Small and elegant Cal Hastings set his smooth-shaven jaws together, recovered his poise, and said to the wireman, "That'll be just fine, thank you."

"Yessir," the wireman said, like a new actor in *Uncle Tom's Cabin*. "You can count on me."

"Good day, Mr. Benbow," Hastings said. "I thought you'd be on your way to California by now."

"Maybe tomorrow," I said. "Have you floated that big pie in the sky yet?"

"The Great Western Meat Products Company is not pie in the sky," he snapped, tipping up on his toes. "I could sue you for slander for suggesting it."

"I didn't mention the name of your company, Mr. Hastings," I said. "You did."

"What exactly is your business, Mr. Benbow?" he rasped out, his broad forehead flushing red.

"I'm kind of a cowboy Johnny Appleseed that goes around advisin' widders and orphans to hang on to their savin's." I grinned, just to make him madder.

"I've had my eye on you for several days, Benbow," he sputtered. "You're walking a fine line."

"I suppose you been readin' my mail, too?" I glanced over at the long-eared telegrapher.

"I'm warnin' you, mister . . ." Hastings stopped himself and then muttered, "No, you're too damn dumb to take a warning."

I looked at the squint-eyed wireman and asked for any messages.

Sullenly he tossed over the yellow sheet that he and Hastings had just been studying.

TWELVE HOURS BEST POSSIBLE. PREGNANT. MARRY ME. MOTHER.

I hid the smile when I read the end of it. The first four words were the real message; the rest was just to throw the nosy parkers off the track.

"Looks like I better be buyin' a weddin' ring," I murmured worriedly, and I watched the wireman's eyes bulge and heard the crack of his pipestem as he bit down.

Out the door in the failing sun I noticed there were no cattle cars at the chutes, and a pall of gloom seemed to hang over the quiet pens.

Around the corner the tally office was just the opposite, with half a dozen cattlemen confabbing noisily on the front porch, their voices angry.

"I can't wait forever out there."

"If my herd gets caught in a norther . . ."

"My hands are mad enough to kick a hog barefooted!"

"It ain't no way to run a railroad. . . ."

Amongst the cattlemen I noticed Arnold Cherry off to one side, keeping to himself, but looking sullen as a sore-headed dog. He caught my glance, but he didn't even nod.

I went on into the office, where Joe McCoy was trying to placate the Baron Alexis Nabokov by raising his hands and patting the air between them gently.

Banker Kennefik stood nearby looking like a big-eyed barn owl.

"The cattle are yours," the baron said heavily, his attention concentrated on McCoy.

"It's close, but not close enough," McCoy said reasonably. "They're mine when they step into the car. Until then they're yours."

"You said I would have the money in full today," the baron growled hoarsely.

"That was based on the assumption the railroad

would continue to send out cattle cars," McCoy said. "For some reason there's a slowdown. Maybe it's Indians, maybe a bridge out—whatever, I can't pay for cattle that are not legally mine yet."

"They are in your pens."

"You may take them out of my pens any time you like and take them back where you got them." McCoy's temper was beginning to fray loose.

"Just what do you mean by that?" the baron roared, looking like he was ready to grab McCoy's gristly neck and throw him a mile or two.

"What's all the hurry?" I asked mildly in the choked silence.

"Ah, Benbow." McCoy let his breath out and turned toward me. "What have you done?"

He looked at me with those piercing hawk eyes and instantly guessed the truth. He took another deep breath as he worked it out, then nodded and said, "You'd better come up with four aces, or you'll be going down the pike with a knot in your tail."

"Mr. McCoy"—I shook my head mournfully—"I'm just a mortal man travelin' through this world of woe, mending pots and pans, fixin' old harnesses, and helpin' out widows, orphans, and speechless immigrants. Why would you talk that way to me?"

"You think he blew up a bridge?" the baron snarled, advancing on me.

"Not me," I said solidly. "I sat up all night with an old friend that mixed up with bad company and got himself kicked around like he'd been tied to the hind end of a mule."

"Skofer?" McCoy asked, eyeing me again.

"Know him, Baron?" I asked. "Skofer Pierpont. Eastern financier?"

"I know him for a fool and a fraud," the baron growled, trying to look taller than me by sucking in his gut.

"Him and me, we go back a ways," I said, and I put my shoulder behind a hard right hook that hit high on his taut belly, square on the solar plexus, paralyzing his diaphragm.

Air gasped out of his open mouth, and he fell like a cold-cocked bull.

"Not in here!" McCoy yelled. "Take it outside, Benbow."

I looked down into the baron's bulging eyes and said, "That's just for starters," then turned on my heel and went out the door.

The cattlemen were not complaining about anything as I went on by and walked along to the high-timbered back fence of the cattle pens.

I felt fine, like this had started out to be a pleasantly productive day, and maybe Skofer and I could get to California on the baron's reward money.

I made the turn at the corner, which put me out of sight of the office and most everybody else in town. It was back here that Clarissa had seen the giant longhorn bull, and it was across the barren ground toward the trees where the Indian women had been stalked, killed, and mutilated.

I eased along the back side, looking into the pens as I went. The first batch were big four- and five-year-olds, still rank and salty, staring out at me between the rails, ready to charge the fence and hook a horn through. I stayed away and walked slow.

About midway I found the drag critters, the ones that had just barely made it up the trail. Some were old and lame, others were dry stock, culls, and weaned calves weighing four to five hundred pounds. They were more for trying to run and hide than charging for a fight, but there was no place in that pen they could hide except behind one another.

I was leaning in through the railings when someone yelled, "Hey! What you doin'?"

I backed off as an old man came forward slowly, the fowling piece in his hands pointed at my middle.

"Just lookin'."

"Lookers ain't allowed," the old guard said. "Mr. McCoy's orders. Nobody gets near this fence at any time, night or day."

"I wasn't goin' to hurt 'em any," I said. "To tell the truth, I just wanted to look at those brands real close."

"Can't be allowed," he said, not quite so firmly.

I saw the tiny red blood vessels in his cheeks and said, "It wouldn't hurt if I looked while you was holdin' that gun on me."

Taking a couple cartwheels from my pocket, I jingled them in my hand.

"You might get a horn through your head," he muttered, eyeing the silver coins. "Serve you right, too."

"That's my lookout," I said. "I'd like to show you my appreciation. . . ."

He held out his left hand, and I dropped the silver into his warped fingers.

"Take a look, but don't forget I'm right behind you," he said softly, looking both ways.

I moved back to the fence and crawled through. The calves didn't worry me near as much as the old cows with long horns. Oftentimes a cow can be meaner'n a bull, especially if she's got a calf by her side.

Moving slowly, I picked a runty short-horned grulla, but I didn't spook him by heading directly for him. I let him think I was after a black heifer next to him, and when he jumped one way I jumped the other, wrapped my arms around his head, and threw him.

I had him bulldogged down, all right, but his brand was underneath. I twisted him down hard until he figured it was permanent, then quick-like let loose, grabbed his hind hocks, lifted them off of the ground, and put my boot on his shoulder.

A cow can't get up except by starting with the back legs first, so I had him under control until he started kicking and bawling. I leaned over the pink scar that showed a disk with a handle and tried to see if anything showed underneath or if maybe part of another brand happened to stick out enough to see.

Whoever had slapped that brand on had held it plenty long enough to cook anything underneath it. I thought they were lucky they hadn't lost the whole herd to screwworms boring into those raw burns.

About then the steer got a hoof loose and kicked me in the knee, and I let him go.

Limping back toward the fence, I looked at the others, but the man with the branding iron had made no mistakes, at least on these critters.

When I climbed up over the top rail of the fence I saw that the old man had gone.

Something out of somewhere smacked my head, and as I pitched on over the fence I thought I heard the distant boom of a rifle.

I woke up staring at a familiar white-painted ceiling, and instead of Skofer lying on the cot and me sitting on the chair watching, it was the other way around.

Thunder echoed in my ears, and a steady-slugging eight-pound hammer pounded on the hollow log just back of my eyes.

I reached up and gingerly touched the bandage on my head, looked at Skofe, and murmured, "Bush-whacked?"

"Long range. Some old guy found you lying next to the cow pens."

"When?"

"About an hour ago," Skofer said, looking at his tin watch. "An inch over and I'd'a had to plant you, but as it is you'll have the scar haired over in a month or so."

"Why'd anybody want to shoot a saintly old brown-bread eater like me?" I asked.

"Probably figured you aren't as saintly as you think," he said with a cackle.

Doc Shreich moved up close and took my pulse.

"Elevated," he said, "but that's normal under the

circumstances. You would be wise to leave town, Mr. Benbow. This is the second time you've damaged your head—"

"I didn't do it," I said.

"It seems you're asking for it, though." He looked at me over the top of his specs. "Third time is the charm, they say."

"I'll be ever so happy to leave this town, Doc," I said, "just as soon as I get a couple things straightened out."

"But don't you see? Someone doesn't want you meddling and will kill to stop you." He spoke as if I were in the second grade and at the bottom of the class.

"It works both ways, Doc," I said, slowly swinging my legs around and planting my boots on the floor.

"Go slow," he said, "you'll have a dizzy spell."

I already had the dizzy spell, and I waited for it to go away.

"Skofe," I said, "we've got less than twelve hours to settle the baron's business, and the clock is runnin'."

Before I could get to my feet the front door banged open, and Kennefik stalked through the anteroom and strode erectly toward me.

"Ah, Mr. Benbow!" he cried out in joyful surprise, like he hadn't expected to see me alive. "I'm so glad you're not injured seriously."

He took off his plug hat, showing his thin hair brushed forward, looked around coldly at Skofer and the doc, and said, "It's urgent I have a private conference with Mr. Benbow."

I was about to say I kept no secrets from Skofer, but Doc said, "It's time for my afternoon toddy. Would you care to join me, Mr. Haavik?"

"I don't mind if I do," Skofer said, running his tongue over his dry lower lip.

As soon as the door closed behind them Kennefik leaned toward me and asked harshly, "Did you stop those trains?"

I spread my arms wide and said, "Look at me, Kennefik. I couldn't stop an old oxcart."

"There is something very serious going on in this town that I don't know about. You appear to be the darky in the woodpile, so to speak."

"Quit while you're ahead," I said.

"I cannot quit," Kennefik said harshly, and I noticed his jowly face was pale as suet. "I have bought a large amount of stock in the Great Western, and I have loaned the full value of the Frying Pan herd to Baron Nabokov."

"So he's just about cleaned you out. I wonder what he's waitin' around for."

"There are other wealthy men in this town who want to see the meat packing industry flourish here."

"So he's goin' to hold his nerve and suck up every last penny you gents are forcin' onto him."

"There are some things I don't understand," he said bitterly, "and one of them is who you are and where you get your information."

"I'm lookin' for a share in all that money you're throwin' around."

"A simple sharper? I wonder," he said skeptically.

"You can wonder all day, but I've got things to do."

"Hold on a minute." Kennefik started to grab my arm as I stood up and then thought better of it. "If you're simply interested in easy money, I can pay."

"Pay for what?" I asked, waiting for the second dizzy spell to pass.

"I will give you fifty dollars right now just to learn why the cattle trains are delayed. Another fifty to know why you've been involved in the squaw killings. Another fifty to know why you were in the cattle pens today—"

"Sounds like I'm goin' to get rich on my talent for talkin'," I said. "Only my mind's numb from bein' banged around so much."

"I'll double it." Kennefik stared up at me, his fluffy sideburns quivering and putting out puffs of talcum powder.

"I'll tell you this much," I said carefully, "you're not playin' money games with poor folks. The boys that you're figurin' to tie up with drafts and notes and contracts don't play by your rules. They kill people like you. Get out while you're still alive."

"There's still some law in this town," he blustered, "and it's on my side."

"You want it both ways. You want to copper your bets and make a profit either way it goes," I said, moving slowly across the room, fighting to keep my balance. Even then I had to grab the central table to stay upright. "Better to leave the money and save your life."

"I think I've learned what I wanted." A smile suddenly bloomed on his toady white features. "You're just what they've all said, a nosy gunman looking for some easy cash."

"I turned down the easy cash," I muttered, seeing two of his faces slowly merge into one.

"The point is you haven't got the power to stop those trains," he said wisely, "and if you're a brand inspector, you're a long way from home."

"Whatever you say." I nodded and walked back toward the cot again. I made better time, and I didn't weave around as much. All it takes is practice.

"If you want to work for us as a gunman, we may have a place for you," Kennefik said, not listening to me.

"You in on ambushin' me this afternoon?" I asked quietly, hoping he'd show something.

"Not in any way, shape, or form," he declared too quickly.

I walked toward the door that led into the anteroom with the banker following me along, berating me for passing up such a golden opportunity. My head started to spin again, and I leaned against the wall so hard the framed medical degrees rattled back at me.

I looked at them blearily, waiting for the world to catch up.

Gunther Shreich
Doctor of Medicine
University of Heidelberg

Gunther Shreich
Progenitive Pathologist
University of London

Gunther Shreich
Doktor der Philosophie
University of Berlin

"Are you all right?" the banker purred so smoothly it scared me, and I moved quickly away from the wall.

"Sure," I said. "You still here?"

"I am here." I saw his pale face swimming up at me, a thin smile on his rattlesnake lips. "You really ought to lie down a while longer."

I wondered what had bothered me. Something in the purring silkiness of his voice.

"Good idea," I said, and I wandered back toward the cot against the far wall.

As I went by him I heard a metallic click that I'd heard at other odd times and dropped to the floor as a very small gun made a very big explosion, spewing smoke and unburned powder and something bigger than a forty-five-caliber bullet where I'd just been.

Blindly I rolled under the table, and the paunchy banker threw the empty derringer at my head and drew another.

As I crawled out the other side of the table I palmed my own forty-four, veered to one side, and rolled again as he fired. This one burned between my arm and upper ribs as I came up from my roll and shot him in his neat little alderman paunch.

He threw up his arms and staggered backward, his face contorted, his toad mouth open.

As his back flattened against the wall he put his hands down to his waist and felt the drainage.

"How?" he groaned as his knees let loose and he slid down to a sitting position.

"Why?" I asked, getting to my feet again.

"You were in the way," he groaned with his eyes closed tightly.

"In the way of you losin' all your money?" I was mystified. I had been trying to save his money for him. He should have been on my side.

"The money is gone, lost. The baron led me into some bad investments." He smiled tightly and shuddered. "I'm the Judas leading the lambs."

"The baron promised you a percentage if you vouched for the Great Western?"

He didn't need to nod.

"Doctor!" he screamed.

The scummy, bloody puddle widened around him. Suddenly he knocked the back of his head against the wall and screamed again.

I reloaded and faced him. "Do you know who's responsible for killin' those Indian ladies?"

"No!" he shrieked. "Get the doctor!"

I didn't tell him that a doctor couldn't save him or anybody else with perforated intestines.

"Sure, be glad to," I said, finding my hat and heading slowly for the door.

"No! Stay with me!" he screamed at my back.

I kept on going. I didn't like the smell.

Outside on the street a group of the curious-minded were gathering.

"We heard some shots." A skinny lady wearing a hat piled high with wax fruit and feathers stared at me. "Is the doctor in?"

"No," I said, touching my hat politely, "the banker is in, but the doctor is out."

"Is he dead?" a storekeeper in a denim apron asked seriously.

"Close enough," I said, and I started to push through the crowd when Fred Keogh appeared in front of me.

"Let's go back in," he drawled.

"It isn't lilacs in May," I said, turning back.

"It never is," he said as he closed the door against the crowd.

I let him go ahead to the back room and look at Kennefik drumming the floor with the heels of his calfskin boots.

"How come?" Keogh asked.

"He had two hideouts. Big bastards. He thought I was too dizzy to beat him."

Keogh gathered up the pair of fifty-one-caliber derringers, sniffed their barrels, and pocketed them.

"Nick you?" he asked.

"Creases," I said, touching the two spots on my right side. "Ruined a good shirt," I added, looking at the blood on my fingertips.

"You seem to attract trouble," he said. "Mind tellin' me why?"

"I think my mother was struck by lightning just before I was born." I shook my head. "But in this case you better look for the baron if you want the troublemaker."

"The baron couldn't have killed all them squaws," Keogh said softly.

"That's right," I admitted. "That was somebody else."

"You know who?" Keogh came up with a question I didn't want to hear.

"I can make a guess, but not right now."

"It's some risky holdin' back," he said, his sardonic gray eyes boring in.

"I've got to make sure I'm right."

"Do you think it's me?" he asked.

"Deputy Keogh, if I did, I sure wouldn't tell you," I said, heading for the door.

I looked in the Long Branch and the New Elephant for Doc and Skofer, but all I found was fun-loving cowboys trying to out-horseplay each other. Some were so drunk the sporters wouldn't dance with 'em, so they were dancing together, slamming their heels down hard and ki-yi-ing like Comanches.

Hell, I thought, they're old enough to look out for themselves, and I stopped in the Gilded Clown for a drink of Tennessee's best.

I stayed down at the end of the bar with my back to the wall, about as far out of harm's way I could get, and was enjoying the warmth in my stomach rising up through my chest.

A couple drinks of good whiskey is a blessing to a man with sore muscles and big problems in his head, but you can't go past that two or three. Three means you aren't usin' it, it's usin' you.

I felt so good, I thought that clear brown whiskey might even explain that little bee buzzing in the back of my head, trying to tell me something I needed to know, or maybe already knew but wasn't looking at it right. It was kind of like looking into two mirrors; you can't ever quite catch the real image of yourself no matter how quick you peek.

It wasn't even dark yet, but the cowboys were standing tall and carrying on like a bunch of outlaws escaped from a lunatic asylum.

Drowsily I reckoned I ought to start looking for Skofer when I saw ex–Major Frederick Hawes and the redheaded trooper wearing the insignia of the Seventh Cavalry enter and elbow their way up to the bar. I recognized the trooper as the one Hawes hung out with most of the time.

I wondered if the Seventh was still over at Fort Hays, or whether this one had been left behind on special duty. Maybe Tom Custer was coming around in the dark of the night to visit the river camp with his scalping knife.

They drank two fast clear ones and seemed amused by whatever they were cooking up. Once in a while Hawes would glance over his shoulder, but he couldn't see around the big peeler in front of me.

I followed along as they went on out to the boardwalk and headed directly for the mercantile. I stayed outside and looked through the display window, which featured back-to-school specials including harmonicas at twelve cents apiece, sets of dominoes at ten cents, slingshots at seven cents apiece, lead pencils, three cents apiece, slates, eight cents apiece, whistles for four cents, and Jew's harps for seven cents apiece.

The major and the redheaded trooper went into the back of the store and presently came out carrying a stoneware gallon jug.

Once they cleared the crush of cowboys the major pulled a flask from under his tunic and offered the trooper a drink, then had a solid jolt himself.

Staggering some, they took the shortcut by the cattle pens and crossed the open field toward the river camp where small campfires glowed through the dusk.

They never looked back. They had two more solid drinks from the flask before they reached the trees.

I circled around to the river, and, staying in the timber, worked my way around so that I could hear what these jolly, intoxicated soldiers had on their penny-apiece minds.

There were more flabby old men than squaws, and when they heard the major whoop, "Come on everybody, let's have a drink!" the camp came out of its stupor, and a dozen Indians staggered toward the fire.

They stood in blank amazement as the trooper lifted the salt-glazed jug and pulled out the corncob stopper.

Sniffing the corncob, he smiled. "Good stuff!"

"Heap good," the major said wetly. "Drink?"

He handed the jug over to a very old squaw, but the one-eyed chief grabbed it away from her before she could take a drink.

I didn't like any part of it, if only because it didn't add up.

"Hold it," I murmured, coming out of the dark trees, my hand on the butt of my forty-four.

"What the hell!" the redheaded trooper mumbled, and he started backing off.

"I said hold it," I repeated with more authority, and he stopped.

The derelicts backed off when I took the jug from the chief.

"What are you givin' away to your ancient enemies, Major?" I asked, hooking my thumb in the handle and taking a whiff.

"Go ahead." The major's voice was wet and slurred, his eyes owlish. "It's pure alcohol cut to a hundred proof."

It smelled like alcohol, which bothered me all the more. I'd thought it might be some sweet sarsaparilla laced with arsenic or castor oil, but it wasn't anything except alcohol, just like the major said.

I tilted it up on my forearm and let a drop touch my tongue. It burned just the way clear stuff would.

"What's the joke, Major?" I asked. "Why do you want them any drunker than they are?"

"What have you got against folks havin' a good time?" he countered slowly, trying to speak every word correctly.

"Major, I've had a low score today. So far I've only got one corpse to my credit, and I need two more to get my discount from the gravedigger."

"You smelled it . . . you tasted it . . ." His makeshift smile was sodden. "Take it. Do whatever you want with it. We're leavin'."

"You put strychnine in this?" I asked bluntly. "Arsenic? Paregoric?"

"You would taste any of those." He shook his blocky head slowly. "Go ahead, you've made your play, now you can give the party."

"I don't want you to leave so soon, Major," I said, jacking back the hammer of the forty-four.

That seemed to get some of their ossified attention, and they quit edging away from the campfire.

"Come on back here where I can see you better," I said, trying to figure what dirty trick they had planned.

I passed over the jug to the wavering major with my left hand and said, "You take the first drink."

"Fine with me," he muttered, tilting the jug up to his mouth. I watched his Adam's apple.

It didn't move. He was only burning his lips.

"God, that's good." He exhaled with his mouth open loosely. A few tiny drops flew off his mustache and fell toward the fire, where they popped into quick blue sparks and were gone.

"You next, trooper," I said, still puzzled.

The trooper pretended a little too much. He bulged his eyes, made a big grin, and slurred, "Boy, howdy, I could drink that good clear all night long."

The worried derelicts moved back when the trooper passed the jug over to the major.

"Go ahead—if you're man enough," the major sneered, and he held the swaying jug out toward me with both hands. I extended the index finger of my left hand toward him, keeping my eyes on both of them.

In the flickering light he fumbled drunkenly as he tried to hang the jug on my finger.

"Just tell me," I said, trying to see into his owly eyes, "is it pure clear whiskey, or is it pure wood alcohol?"

The jug handle missed and slid by my extended index finger, and I knew he was going to drop it.

"Look out!" I yelled, making a mighty grasshopper leap off to the side, and hugging the ground as the jug fell toward the rock-ringed fire.

A blue and white bomb went off.

Bouquets of bluebonnets from hell, blue, white, and molten red sprayed up from the fire.

Poof . . . *boom!* I saw the blue explosion just as the shock punched me flat on my face.

Shapes of Indians crawled away as I shook my head, trying to clear my mind and unplug my ears.

Maybe deafness was better.

Howling like a dying dog, ex–Major Frederick Hawes writhed in the exploded campfire with pale blue flames licking around his blackened chest and neck and face. The trooper had been blown backwards, but the front of his tunic was burned off, and his body was afire with ghostly bluish flames that were almost invisible and intensely hot.

The major was a hopeless case. I grabbed a blanket off a crawling buck and covered the trooper with it, putting out the fire.

Gasping for air, he coughed hoarsely until a spasm

shuddered through his body. He'd breathed in the ghostly fire, and he was beyond pain anymore.

I dragged the major clear of the embers.

He'd meant to blind, paralyze, or kill the entire camp of outcasts with that jug. I couldn't feel sorry for him as I gazed down into the char of a face that once, long, long ago, had belonged to a man.

— 12 —

I THOUGHT I HEARD SKOFER CALLING MY NAME, AND I awakened in the darkness, ready to fight, but there was no sound in the room, not even Skofer's snoring. I lighted a phosphor and saw that his bed hadn't been slept in.

Not important, really. Likely he was in a different bed snuggled up to a swamp amazon.

I looked out the dark window and saw the palest pink glow to the east, and as I slipped on my boots and hat I grumbled to myself about how some old coots get to frolic while the rest of us honest souls have to work.

It was still close on dark when I went out through the vestibule into the street. Delmonico's was closed. The whole street was closed. No coffee.

Still half asleep, I went over to the livery stable and saddled up the steeldust, led him outside, and mounted up.

The anguished whistle of a train wailed from far across the prairie, and I knew my twelve hours of grace were about used up, and the baron's herd would soon be eastward bound.

From thinking about him and his stolen cows that I could do little about, I thought of McCoy's missing steers. Had the baron lost any yearlings in the night? How did the boatman manage his pilferage? I pushed away the other thought about the river camp, its misery, its grisly murders. The major and the trooper were enough to last me a couple of lifetimes. I didn't want to go near the place again.

I rode across the tracks and headed for the river, the steeldust all but prancing for joy to get out of the boredom of his stall. He flicked his heels in a fancy way of going, arched his neck, and neighed at shadows.

At the timber-lined riverbank I turned him downstream, guessing that a skiffload of beef would be too hard to row against the current.

The freight train called again across the pale pink prairie: Hurry . . . look alive . . . hurry . . . look alive. . . .

"Goddammit, I'm hurryin'," I growled grouchily, wishing now I'd found a cup of coffee someplace before starting out.

I didn't know where to hurry to. I was just following a hunch that those missing critters had somehow been carried to the boat across that empty field and that the boat had gone downstream with the current. There had been two sets of prints in the mud, but I couldn't see how two people could carry a six-hundred-pound critter across that field, and for damn sure the critter didn't walk.

The burning rim of the sun melted the blue eastern horizon and turned the morning into pale lavender light, a hazy dreamland that stretched away forever and beyond. I wished I could gather it up in my hands and bottle it so that on a raw winter day in the midst of a blue norther I could take down a bottle and pour it all over the kitchen table until it spread out and filled the room with the color of lilac blossoms.

"Good Christ!" I said out loud. "You're gettin' soft in the head, Sam. Straighten yourself up and get your mind on business."

But that was the problem; the business so far had been mostly killing people the hard way, and my mind was so sick of blood it wanted to think of hazy sunrises and drooping, dew-laden lilac blossoms.

The steeldust splashed across the river, alert and eager to run, but I turned him east again as soon as we crossed and stayed close to the timber.

I was willing to take anything I could get. A sound of an axe, a telltale whiff of smoke, even the wagon tracks that crossed a fan of silt left by the last flood, two straight grooves with the prints of two horses pulling. Probably a buckboard.

It had come down this way and gone back often

enough in the past few weeks to have worn its own trail through the brush and green grass.

Where I was headed I wasn't exactly sure, but I was confident that I wouldn't be welcomed.

Holding the steeldust to a cautious walk, I kept my eyes peeled for a surprise, then I caught a brassy sparkle off to my left and ducked low.

A heavy-caliber bullet howled through the space my head had just occupied. I kneed the steeldust and whirled him into a stand of cottonwoods, dragged out my carbine, and hit the ground.

There were two of them, I told myself, and they knew the ground a lot better than I did. Their camp had to be close by, and I wanted to see it.

Times like that, you have to go very slow, but you have to break it up with short sprints and a sliding dive or they'll pin you down. It gets to be a guessing game, and you have to be more than good at it; you have to be lucky.

Someone had an idea of where I was, but I had seen nothing but the glint of a brass-framed rifle.

I crawled along on my belly to reach a fallen cottonwood log and took a quick peek through a few dead limbs, saw nothing, ducked back. The responding bullet cut through the dead branches overhead.

He was very good. He knew his business about as well as or better than I knew mine.

I moved to the end of the log, poked out my hat, and got a rifle ball through it instantly.

This was not the place to make a sprint, I decided, and I crawled to the other end where I could work through a tangle of chokecherries and wild sand-hill plums, which offered no protection against a high-velocity 450-grain hunk of lead punching through.

I angled to my right to the base of an old walnut, counted one, and jumped across the open space to the shelter of a low bank.

From there I'd have to cross open ground to reach a cottonwood, and I didn't like the odds. I crawled the other way, and as I poked my head out to look another bullet buzzed by my ear. It looked like I'd have to move back through the chokecherries and try another route.

Or I could just ramble back to Dodge, climb into a warm, cozy bed, and dream about the good old days.

Before I made up my mind a voice behind me said, "That's it, Benbow. Drop it." Cussing myself, I let loose of the carbine and got up on my knees.

"Before you turn around, shuck that gunbelt."

I unbuckled and laid the belt and six-gun by the butt of the carbine, then turned around. Maric knelt by the bole of an ancient ash tree, his six-gun pointed at my midsection. His bearded visage was set, his eyes alert and ready for action.

"Don't think about it," he said. "You're good, but you're not perfect."

"I'd as soon say you're better. I've forgot some things." I nodded.

"Hold your fire, Suzie!" he yelled. "We're comin' in.

"Go ahead," he said to me. "No tricks and you might live."

As I walked toward the river he gathered up my weapons and followed along close behind.

"I didn't come out to shoot anybody," I said.

"You figured you could take me alive?" Maric's voice sounded amazed. "You been a mountain-man trapper. How'd you like to be chained and locked up in an iron box?"

"I haven't thought that far ahead," I said as we came into a small clearing that was surrounded on three sides by big trees. On the fourth side the Arkansas River flowed by ever so gently, and an old flat-bottomed rowboat had been dragged up on the bank.

To one side an oiled tarp was tied in the trees to make a lean-to, and blankets were spread out underneath.

A rock-lined firepit hadn't been lighted yet. Thin strips of salted meat were hung out on twine strings to dry.

"Regular jerky factory," I commented.

"If we have to walk to the mountains, we'll need that and more," Maric said. "Set over on that log and don't do nothin' crazy."

"I'm not goin' to look even cross-eyed so long as your partner is out there with a bead on my backbone," I said, doing as he advised. "Suppose we could have a fire and make some coffee? I started out a little early."

"Not now," he said, his voice hard with certitude, his face a solid mask of determination. "We parley first. How'd you figure it?"

"I don't know much yet," I said, "but I went through a list in my head of gents who could make a young steer disappear from a well-made cattle pen, and there was only one man around town that I could think of. Then I remembered Spud the butcher looked prosperous."

"He gave me a few dollars for the choice cuts, but never enough to break us loose," Maric said. "But how did you figure this place?"

"Mary, the squaw, showed me where you landed the boat. I read your prints." I shrugged. "I guessed downriver."

"Now," Maric said, frowning and speaking slowly, "just tell me what's your interest in my business."

"I'm a brand inspector up from Texas on another case, but then a couple days ago McCoy missed some young stuff."

"Damn," Maric said bitterly. "We took so few and cleaned up so good, I was hopin' he'd blame it on his bookkeeper."

"It was just a fluke that I was standin' there when he checked his tally and it made him mad."

"Now I suppose I have to tie a rock around your neck and see if you can swim downriver," Maric muttered.

"There must be a better way," I said carefully.

"The other day I figured you as bein' savvy and honest. I just don't see how to get around that and still keep my freedom."

"Tell me how you did it," I said, trying to gentle him down and keep him away from hasty decisions.

"It wasn't easy"—he shook his head—"but I was backed into a corner and had no choice. I'd sneak over there to the pens with a six-pound hammer. It's not so hard for a trapper to slip in with a bunch of young cattle and brain one.

"The hard part was dragging him under the fence and gutting him out so that we could carry him on a pole over our shoulders. It took two trips and one extra to sweep dirt over the blood."

"The night guards?"

"Was just one. He was too drunk to walk after midnight," Maric said. "It was just a lot of hard work."

"What'd you do with the hides?"

"Hides, heads, hocks, and guts all fed the catfish."

"Damn," I said, disappointed. "Main reason I came out was to look at the hides."

"Why?"

"I need evidence against a man."

"Right now you don't have any evidence against me," he said, "except maybe that jerky."

"That jerky don't carry a brand," I said, "and what you told me you can change."

"You believe my story about tryin' to get back to the far places?" he asked, looking me square in the eye.

"You know I do because I know the life there."

He thought about it awhile, then stood up, turned his back on me, and yelled out to the woods, "Susie! Come in!"

Turning back, he shrugged his shoulders and said, "Did I tell you that she followed me afoot to Missouri? Wouldn't leave. Threw rocks at her, but she wouldn't go. We're in it together."

She led in my steeldust and carried the old rifle at the ready. She wore buckskins, and worn-out brogans on her feet.

She was broad-faced, and the braids of her black hair fell to her waist. Still a handsome woman, she had only one thing on her mind, and that was to stay with her man and help him any way she could.

"This is Benbow, the man I told you about," he said to her.

She leaned the rifle against a log and stood in front of me, gazing up into my face, searching out the leftovers of the past. Then she touched my cheek with her right hand and said, "Welcome to this camp."

Compared to the derelicts upriver, she was so alive and beautiful in her humanness I felt a fresh wonder rise up in my mind at how people can surprise you by their simple goodness, a wonder that had been eroding away in the past months and years, day by day, person by person.

But that sincerity on her plain face, that sureness of what life must be no matter what, brought it back, and I was grateful.

"I am much obliged," I said.

Maric coughed and cleared his throat like he was strangling, and when he finally got his voice box going he said, "Benbow, we made a run last night, and we didn't get finished because you came along crashing through the brush like a gang of Chinese track layers."

"You've still got the hide?" I asked.

No wonder he'd been nervous. Close by was evidence enough to hang both of them.

"C'mon," he growled, and he led me off into the timber where a young beef hung from improvised gambrel hooks.

It had been gutted out and the head cut off, leaving about a three-hundred-pound carcass. The black hide with a yellow line stripe down the backbone was still in place. The brand on the left hindquarter was the Frying Pan.

"There's your hide, but it won't tell you nothin' you don't already know," he said. "I was just fixin' to peel it off."

"Go ahead," I said, smiling, "maybe we can learn a new way to skin a cat."

He'd already made his cuts down the inside of the legs to the crotch and, stepping close to the hanging carcass, he grabbed a flap of hide at the knee and jammed his thumb between hide and meat. When he had made room enough he worked his fist in between, pulling down all the time with his left hand.

He was strong and fast, and he fisted off the hide expertly without getting any hair on the meat.

Susie reached up and worked on the other hind leg alongside him, and together they fisted the hide down to the neck in a couple of minutes. The neck was too tough for fisting, and he let Susie use the skinning knife to trim it off.

As she made her final cut I grabbed the tail and pulled the hide clear of the dark red carcass with yellow tallow along the backbone.

Dragging the hide back into camp, I stretched it out over a log, flesh side out.

The Frying Pan scar was hard and showed through, but the clear tracery of the Terrazas brand was an indelible part of it.

"I'll be go to hell," Maric said.

"That's what I've been lookin' for," I said.

"So the baron stole a whole goddamned herd?"

"They found the bodies of the vaqueros across the border," I said with a nod.

"So you ain't so awful worried about somebody that ain't killed anybody nor stole a whole damn herd," Maric said.

"You might even be in for part of the reward," I said.

When Susie joined us I took her hand and said, "Thank you. I wish you good luck.

"Can I have this old hide I found downriver?" I asked Maric, folding the hide into a neat bundle.

"Hell, yes," he said. "It sure ain't mine."

"I'll be back," I said, stowing the hide in my saddlebags and mounting up.

"You can come along with us over beyond the shining mountains," Maric said. "We wouldn't bother you none."

"Not just yet, thanks," I said, kneeing the steeldust through the trees.

I heard the mournful plaint of the cattle train as it

approached Dodge, and I set the steeldust to doing what he'd been wanting to do all morning: splitting the wind.

By the time we crossed the river he was settling down to a long lope, and by the time we crossed the railroad tracks he was content with a high-headed trot.

The cattle cars were parked on the tracks next to the chutes, and on down at the tally office a bunch of men was gathering around the baron.

I lifted my six-gun from its holster and checked the loads just in case Maric had ejected them, then I put a sixth brass cartridge under the hammer and slid the Colt back into its scabbard.

Coming closer, I noticed McCoy and his clerk standing out on the porch with the Frying Pan crew. The clerk held the handle of a valise that was mighty heavy, or he was awful puny.

"A sight draft will be a lot easier to carry and just as easy to bank as gold," McCoy was saying as I stopped at the hitch rail.

"I like hard money." The baron glared at McCoy. "Let's get it over with."

"Technically the cattle aren't loaded yet, but the cars are here now, and there's no point in making you wait the extra day," McCoy said, then he looked over at me and shrugged his shoulders.

"Thank you," Hastings said, reaching for the valise.

I glanced at the hardcases in the Frying Pan crew, idly resting here and there. A couple of them leaning on the hitch rail made room for the steeldust, and another couple squatted down on the backs of their boots, making marks in the dirt with twigs.

"Wait a minute," I said.

Changing my mind about putting the steeldust right there, I reined him over to the cattle pen and, dismounting, hauled off my saddlebags and bowlegged it back to the porch.

I felt some better when I saw Fred Keogh standing tall just inside the door. I gave him a hard look, then put my back to the wall, opened the saddlebag, hauled out the wet black hide, and spread it out.

"That's off one of my cattle," the baron said sharply.

"I found it down by the river," I said.

"What's one out of three thousand?" short, erect, leonine Cal Hastings said, reaching for the valise again.

"What are you doing, Benbow?" McCoy snapped, exasperated.

I nudged the hide over with the toe of my boot so it was flesh side out. "Don't that look like a T R S connected on the inside?" I asked quietly, stepping back until I felt the wall comforting my shoulder blades.

"That's a Mexican brand," McCoy said slowly, trying to figure out what was going on.

"Of course," the baron said strongly. "The Frying Pan is our road brand."

"Then I'll have to see your bill of sale from the

Mexican," McCoy said slowly, anger and doubt showing on his hawk face.

"Mexicans don't give bills of sale," Hastings said smoothly. "You pay them the money, and you take possession of the cattle. Very simple."

"I'm not partial to blotted brands," McCoy said, "Mexican or otherwise."

"You don't think I'd bother to steal a small herd of cattle when I own a million-dollar company, do you?" the baron said with a laugh.

"I do," I said. "It's over, Baron, finished. That double brand tells no lies."

"That's a very serious charge," Hastings protested, backing off.

"Mr. McCoy," I said, "better you and that bright lad carry your money back inside and put it in a safe place."

The Frying Pan hands spoke in laconic undertones and pretended to be disinterested in the proceedings in spite of a damning wet cowhide lying there in plain sight. I noticed a bluebottle fly circle over it and settle down for dinner.

As McCoy and the clerk moved toward the door Keogh stepped aside to let them pass, making the moment the others were waiting for.

A stumpy, swarthy gunsel at the end of the hitch rail moved first, quick and eager. I cleared leather a whisker ahead of him and punched dust out of his vest twice, then swung over to my right, where Hastings was lifting his arm, the immaculate gray worsted coat sleeve stretching as his right hand rose with the palm up in a sign of peace.

I jerked back and slammed a bullet between his fragile ribs as the sleeve gun went off, scorching my chest with its heavy slug.

As he fell I wheeled to one side, breaking up the set picture for them, and snapped two more shots at the hands who'd been hunkered down off to the right.

There wasn't time to aim, take a bead, line a man up, then squeeze slow. Not now. The pair to the side weren't dead, but they were hurt enough to stumble away, hunting a hole.

The fourth gunsel was slow but steady; his Colt was rising, and he was sighting over the notch and blade like his mother had told him to always put everything in its place and always do a good job no matter how long it took you.

My shot ripped through the throat and blew his neck bones out the back, and he never finished the good job he meant to do.

The baron had moved close and fingered out a two-bore wide-barreled derringer as I swung the forty-four around at him and dropped the hammer on a spent cartridge.

"Don't!" I heard Keogh yell, but the baron wasn't listening. As he brought up the deadly derringer and shoved it against my chest Keogh's shot roared in my ear, and a reddish-blue hole appeared in the bulging left temple of the baron's forehead. Time froze on his face. His eyelids widened, his eyes died, his nerves stopped, and the derringer clattered to the floor a second before his bulk slowly toppled like a felled pine tree.

Not hesitating, I was ejecting brass and thumbing fresh blunt-headed cartridges from my belt when Keogh said, "No hurry, Benbow. Looks like you swept the board." I stared at him, not knowing truly where he stood.

"Worried, ain't you?" He chuckled thinly and carefully holstered his piece, adding, "No need."

"Much obliged," I said, clicking the cylinder back in place and setting the six-gun in its holster.

"You reckon they got the million?" Keogh asked, looking away from the carnage.

"Whatever they swindled from the gulls, they didn't take it along," I said. "Maybe Mr. McCoy can straighten it out."

"Goddammit, Benbow," McCoy snapped angrily, coming out the door. "How can I even sort out this Mexican herd of cows, let alone straighten out the rest of this devilment!"

"Load 'em and sell 'em," I said. "Commander Frasier will get the money to the Terrazas."

"You been working against me all along, haven't you?" McCoy gritted out angrily. "I've been sweating blood waiting for those empty cars."

"Part of the game." I shrugged. "Anybody seen Skofer?"

"Last night he was playing the piano over at Polly's," Keogh said.

I felt the blood oozing down my leg from a wound I didn't know anything about until just then, and I figured I'd better get along.

"Maybe I'll mosey over that way," I said.

"Wait a goddamn minute!" McCoy roared. "What

am I going to do with all this?" He spread his hands out to indicate the sprawled, grotesque bodies.

"Talk to Deputy Keogh, Mr. McCoy," I said. "He'll give you a discount if there's enough volume."

I limped over to the steeldust and found it a little tender putting my weight on the near stirrup as I swung aboard.

"Wait a second," McCoy roared again. "You're bleeding!"

I didn't answer but single-footed the steeldust up the street and turned right on Nauchtown trail. In a minute the cribs and Harry's Lucky Horseshoe showed up on my right, and Polly's Palace on down the street.

The quietness of the house bothered me, and I rode a circle around the boxy building before dismounting at the back door.

I knocked and called softly for Clarissa, not wanting to disturb the ladies getting their beauty rest upstairs.

I opened the door and walked through the kitchen. The stove lids were cold as death.

A snake of fear ran up my backbone.

I looked in the ballroom, but there was no old coot singing bawdy songs on the piano bench, and no ladies in ruffles and feathers. The air smelled of dead perfume, dead sweat, dead smoke, and dead love.

The eerie silence bothered me worse than seeing that short, swarthy gunsel's six-gun coming up at me, and I went on back outside where the air was better.

Standing on the back steps, I tried to figure my next choice when I noticed the sloping cellar doors weren't closed properly. One was supposed to lap over the other to keep out the rain and snow, but now it was backward, leaving a gap.

I lifted one of the doors and smelled the sweet, sickening smell of ethyl ether.

Leaning the other door against its prop, I went down the stairs into the gloom.

Skofer lay in the corner next to a sack of potatoes. I lifted the pad of cotton from his face.

He was alive. Pale, the old scars even paler. He breathed short, shallow pantings, each one seeming his last. I carried him up the stairs and laid him in the shade where there was a breeze.

Downstairs again I looked at the worst of it. I couldn't.

I charged back up and puked on some weeds. Tears flooded my eyes, and I stood leaning over, gasping. My stomach recoiled again. The saliva quit flowing, but my eyes wouldn't quit watering.

Nothing for it. Got to do it. Benbow will fix it, honor bound.

You say to yourself, yes, you owe her. But, you say, it's already over. You know it all. You could even have prevented it if you'd had the sense of a half-assed jaybird. But there's that old duty sergeant ordering you to go back and look close until you're absolutely sure of yourself, so you walk down those dank stairs again with the tears still flooding from your open eyes, you go over to the table where she folded the laundry, and look down at the rictus of horror on Clarissa's long ebony face, now the color of swamp mud, and you turn her head to see the tiny wound in the nape of her neck. Still weeping silently, your tears falling on her small, hard breasts, you look down at her lower abdomen to see the T cut and evisceration of her sexual organs; then, still blubbering tears, you turn slowly and climb up the stairs again, duty done, sir.

My leg had quit bleeding—I'd forgotten about it—and now the first thing was to tend to Skofer.

I knew what ether was: a new, experimental chemical made from sulfuric acid and ethyl alcohol, highly unstable, capable of putting people out of pain, but an overdose would eat out their lungs.

Whether Skofer had an overdose I had no way of knowing, but listening to his panting chest and looking at the sugar-white wrinkled skin, I had cause to worry.

I hoisted him up on my shoulder and told the steeldust to behave.

I suppose if Skofer weighed over a hundred pounds I couldn't have done it, but I managed to swing into the saddle and ride back up Nauch Street with the little booger hanging over my shoulder.

Crossing the tracks, I turned right at Front Street, and in the next block I turned the steeldust to face the hitch rail. Carefully dismounting, trying not to knock his gray head on the saddle, I walked across the boardwalk and pushed open the door to Doc's anteroom.

Nobody there.

I banged on through the door into the back room, where Doc Shreich sat on a tall stool at the table, bending over the microscope, making quick scribbles in a notebook, his spectacles lying close by.

I carried Skofer over to the familiar cot and laid him down. I thought maybe he was breathing a little better.

"Doc," I said, "Skofer's bad off."

"I'm awfully busy," he said, not moving his eye from the microscope. "Time is critical."

"I don't think it'll wait, Doc."

"Cover him with a blanket und see he doesn't swallow his tongue," Doc said, not looking up, scribbling his notes.

I rolled Skofer onto his side and covered him with an old army blanket.

"That's all?" I asked.

"Please, Mr. Benbow," he protested, his eye still screwed onto the lens, "this is most urgent. I'll be with you in a few minutes."

I walked over to the table. Alongside the microscope the copper-clad keg was hinged open, and in the salt water floated a tangle of pink female genital organs, complete except for a snippet of fallopian tube that he was studying in the microscope. Ovaries, tubes, uterus, vagina, cervix—all soaking quietly in the salt water, waiting for him to slice off another specimen and put it under magnification.

"Clarissa?" I had to ask.

"She was sterile, you know," he murmured, writing quickly in the notebook.

The hair on the back of my neck bristled up, and my hands felt clammy.

"I didn't know—I didn't even care. . . ." I shook my head.

"Unfortunate in a way," he continued quietly. "Still, we'd run out of viable squaws. Next best thing . . . the research too near finishing to quit now . . ."

"But why so many?"

"No refrigeration. No ice. They won't keep."

"I kind of figured Clarissa was a friend of mine."

"Yes, mine, too, but we must make hard decisions," he muttered, poking at the specimen with the point of a scalpel, his eye still fixed against the top of the microscope.

"Likely you didn't ask her permission."

"No time. What is more important? Solve the most difficult problem in the scientific world or worry about a small und unproductive life?"

"I don't think you have the right to choose."

"I suppose if you want to be technical about it, perhaps not. But I know what I'm doing, and you don't." He frowned.

"Doc, you're a murderer."

"When did you first guess?" He nodded slightly.

"Sometime back," I said, "but I wasn't sure until I read your university degrees."

"They are authentic," he murmured.

"Yes, but what's progenitive pathology?"

"The study of deviations from normal sexual reproduction." He smiled.

"Which is what you're doing right now." I nodded.

"Very perspicacious," he said, pulling his half-bald head back and squinting at me owlishly.

His gaze drifted past me, and he said quickly, "I told you to watch the old man didn't swallow his tongue!"

Like a perfect fool listening to a trusted doctor I turned to look, and with perfect, practiced precision he grabbed my hair with his left hand and aimed the scalpel at the back of my neck.

I wasn't thinking about where it was aimed. The moment he touched my hair I was moving.

Lunging away, I pulled him off the stool and kicked backward, my boot heel connecting with his knee.

He let loose of my hair and made a swipe with the scalpel. Off balance I swung an awkward right hand at him, and he ducked and scampered toward the back door, screaming, "I'm almost finished, you fool!"

He'd forgotten the door was locked, and he ran back alongside the far wall, screeching all the while about me interfering with his plan to give all women fertility, babies, families, fulfillment, peace of mind, peace on earth. . . .

"You ignorant lout!" he yelled at me.

I just watched. I didn't consider him a threat anymore. Now it was just a question of waiting for him to run down and then handing him over to Fred Keogh.

"You're sneering!" he shrieked. "You set humankind back five centuries, und you're sneering at me like a Barbary ape!"

"Steady on, Doc. I'm not sneering, and I'm not goin' to hurt you," I said quietly, and I moved toward him. He suddenly stopped babbling.

"You're goin' to have to quit killin' people, Doc," I said soothingly.

A strange expression came over his moon face, and he said, "Give me just five minutes more und I can maintain the continuity."

"It's over, Doc."

"Five minutes," he begged. "Just give me that!"

I shook my head and moved toward him.

The little old guy looked so vulnerable to a veteran like me, I just didn't have a worry in the world until he grabbed the big glass jar of sulfuric acid from the shelf and threw it right at my face.

I caught the move when he turned toward the shelf, drew the forty-four, and yelled, "Don't do it, Doc!"

He was on the warpath and wasn't listening.

My bullet caught him through his squinting left eye as he reached back for another flask of acid.

I dodged away quickly as the jar fell against the side of the table, smashing and spilling its smoking contents to the floor.

Shreich was blown back against the shelves, but there was nothing left in him to hold him up, and he bounced forward, making a slow dive to the floor.

The yellow acid fumed and smoked, bubbled and seethed like a witch's cauldron.

If he hadn't been dead when he fell, I would have shot him for mercy's sake.

By the time I dragged him by his bony little ankle

free of the spuming puddle, there was nothing left of his face but some foaming bone and teeth.

Fred Keogh came trotting in on crotchety bowlegs, six-gun in hand.

He looked over at me, then down at what was left of Doc Shreich, and asked, "What's going on?"

"Bad medicine," I said.

Epilogue

THE CONSTANT PRAIRIE WIND TOUCHED THE COTTON-woods' yellow leaves and carried them off a handful at a time, scattering them like a flurry of butterflies in the soft, winy air. Meadowlarks bulked up with winter's down found southside lees to sing farewell, farewell, and the wild plum tangles in the river bottom assumed the color of clotted blood in the sallow light of autumn.

Maric and Suzie, mounted on stout cow ponies, waited at the fork in the western trail as Skofer and I rode up. Suzie held the cotton lead line of a gray mule packed with all their worldly goods.

"You should be on your way. Winter will be freezin' your butt before you know it," I said, glad, though, that they had waited.

"We are partners," Maric said, looking me in the eye. "It wouldn't be right to go off without a last word."

Suzie looked in even better shape now, more sure, more serene. She'd tied red flannel bows in her long black braids and wore a ring hammered out of a ten-dollar gold piece.

"Let me know next spring how many wagons we'll need to haul out our silver bullion." I smiled.

He reached out his big hand, and I took it in both of mine.

"You're welcome to come along," he said.

"You're livin' a life I enjoyed once, but it's too late now." I shook my head and kneed the steeldust aside.

"Heap thanks," Suzie said to me as Skofer shook hands with Maric.

I thought that sounded so much better'n fuckee-twobits, I almost leaned over and kissed her.

She jerked the lead line, and the mule stepped forward, following along.

"I take it you staked him with our reward money?" Skofer looked at me hard.

"No . . . just your half." I smiled.

"What about our spread in the San Juan Bautista Valley?" he protested.

"First things first," I said, watching the pair, maybe the last of their kind, riding across the long, tawny prairie toward the shining mountains way over yonder.